Doomsday

"Damn it!" Carl Lyons muttered as his CAR-15 jammed on a defective cartridge. With the palm of his hand, he slammed the ejector port several times, but the shell refused to budge—it appeared to have warped immediately after discharge, effectively blocking the breech.

He reached down and drew his commando knife, well aware there would not be enough time to force the cartridge free with the blade's tip. His two Able Team partners were ramming home fresh ammo clips—but he knew they would not be fast enough, either.

This was it.

"Able Team will go anywhere, do anything, in order to complete their mission."
—*West Coast Review of Books*

Mack Bolan's

ABLE TEAM®

ABLE TEAM®
Kill Orbit

Dick Stivers

A GOLD EAGLE BOOK FROM
WORLDWIDE®

TORONTO • NEW YORK • LONDON • PARIS
AMSTERDAM • STOCKHOLM • HAMBURG
ATHENS • MILAN • TOKYO • SYDNEY

Dedicated to Vietnam veterans Francis "Dick" Scobee and Michael J. Smith, and their crew of the Space Shuttle *Challenger*: Ellison Onizuka, Judith A. Resnik, Gregory Jarvis, Ronald McNair and Sharon Christa McAuliffe.

In hopes that January 28, 1986 (which also happened to be the 13th anniversary of the Vietnam ceasefire) shall forever live in the hearts and minds of all Americans. May your ultimate sacrifice not have been in vain.

First edition August 1989

ISBN 0-373-61243-5

Special thanks and acknowledgment to
SGT. NIK-UHERNIK for his contribution to this work.

PROLOGUE

Twenty years ago, when his paycheck was for flying F-4 Phantoms over North Vietnam, Paul "Hawkjaw" Lynch's most famous trademark was his gold-handled .357 Magnum. The six-inch Smith & Wesson and his necklace of Viet Cong molars were legendary. He'd won the revolver from a *canh-sat* policeman in one of Saigon's notorious gambling dens, and "liberated" the molars from the seven Viet Cong unlucky enough to encounter him during his three crash landings behind enemy lines.

The Air Force colonel still remembered how the shiny revolver had dwarfed the Saigon policeman as it rode his hip below the poker table. The *canh-sat* claimed its gold handle was molded from the ceremonial leaf he'd taken off a Buddhist temple in Chieng Mai, and Lynch had no reason to doubt him.

The *canh-sat* had been very upset about losing the revolver. Lynch suspected it was probably doubly insulting to the VNP officer that he lost his prized handgun to a "long-nosed, running dog" foreigner.

Lynch wished he still carried the weapon, but the brass frowned on adding such sentimental accessories to one's official duty uniform. They claimed his Colt .45 was bad enough and preferred he pack an issue .38, but nothing was ever done about his low-key antics. After all, he was one of the walking monuments to the Vietnam War—the last of the Tan Son Nhut gunslingers. He had the grit leg-

ends were made of, the charisma young wing nuts joining
the flight line aspired to imitate. And he was an officer.

Lynch eased the pistol slide back, ejecting the live round
from his .45 Mark IV. He watched the unspent cartridge
float end over end through the air, and plop unceremoniously onto the ground. The graceful, slow-motion arc
ended with a halolike puff of dust that rose from the desert floor.

Dropping into an almost Asian-style squat, the colonel
retrieved the bullet and slipped it into a front pocket.
Since his earliest days wearing the uniform, he'd been a
believer in the locked-and-loaded automatic. Anything
less was unprofessional and could prove quite deadly, he
reasoned. But today was different. He didn't need the
edge—didn't *want* it.

There were opposing forces at war within the career Air
Force officer that humid, hazy afternoon. He wasn't sure
which side would win. And he didn't want any innocent
bystanders paying the ultimate sacrifice because of his
own vice—when there was so little to gain. Especially bystanders wearing blue berets.

It was only when the rain fell hard, as it promised to do
very soon, that he thought of Vietnam. The rain and the
heat lightning brought out the mosquitoes, and they in
turn woke the slumbering memories. That was the only
time he really saw the deadly ridges overlooking Tonkin
Gulf, and the flashes of canon light racing up toward the
clouds, trying to overtake him, to destroy him, the antiaircraft flak bursting all about, attempting to tear his leaf-
colored Phantom apart at the seams, trying to pop the
rivets with earsplitting suddenness, snatch hold, drag him
out of the sky, down into the jungle's unforgiving triple
canopy.

The rain did that to him. And now the trap he had
fallen victim to—a pit far deeper than any punji-laced

ditch he'd encountered in survival camp *or* the rain forests of Indochina—closed in on him, equally vicious and cruel. Equally unforgiving.

Colonel Lynch stood on the ridge overlooking the coastal sector of Vandenberg Air Force Base's Purisima Point. Rain began pelting the poncho liner covering his head and shoulders. A dark blanket of cloud swirled directly above, but in the distance, shafts of sunlight broke through the rolling mist, sending a fan of crimson through the twin rainbows arching over the secret runway. Vandenberg Flight Line Seven.

"So beautiful," Lynch sighed, as he watched a silver speck in the misty distance grow into a bulky yet graceful aircraft. The mock space shuttle touched down on the dry lake bed a half mile away, and silver-blue puffs of smoke billowed almost majestically from beneath its giant tires.

"Beautiful as any bomb blast back in—" The constantly shifting heat waves seemed to split the giant craft down the middle for a moment, silencing him, but then the illusion vanished, and the USS *Specter* became whole again.

The USS *Specter* was not a true space shuttle, of course. Rather, it was a converted AWACs tracking-and-communications ship, a P-3 Orion—specially constructed to not only resemble a smaller version of the shuttle but to perform many of its functions, short of the actual leap from the Earth's upper atmosphere to outer space.

Lynch sighed as he watched the *Specter* roar past—escorted on both sides by smaller, one-man jets bearing Air Force insignia and cloud-white color schemes. Battles. There would always be another battle to fight. "Should be happy..." he muttered, climbing the broken shale cliff for a better vantage point of the hectic operations taking place on the desert plateau below. Should be happy that a warrior in the peacetime armed forces of the greatest nation on Earth still found battles to fight.

"Hold it right there!" a gruff, husky voice called out behind him.

"Hands over your head!" another man warned. "Keep 'em where we can see 'em at all times, or you're dust on the desert wind, mister!"

The words carried no compassion and zero leniency. Lynch could feel both speakers' determination drilling through the back of his head like an air-powered spike hammer: young men with hundreds of hours of training under their belts, too many Rambo movies for motivation and perhaps six months on the firearms range. But they'd had no one to test their skills against, to prove their marksmanship to each other. Until now.

Now they had something, someone to vent their frustrations on. And although Lynch's cockiness had often gotten him the rabbit slot in foot pursuits during POW camp escape-and-evasion training, he no longer enjoyed being in the killing zone—a moving target of opportunity.

These boys carried live ammo in their M-16s and harbored lethal attitudes.

The colonel dropped into a combat crouch and rolled hard to his right, out of the line of fire. He expected to hear automatic rifle discharges and hot lead zinging off shale, but the only sounds filling his ears were his own groans as he tumbled down through the bushes and boulders, and the running boots of several excited security policemen trying to catch up with him.

Five somersaults later he was halfway down the ravine and searching for landmarks. The three-pronged cactus with an empty, bullet-riddled coffee can propped on one of its drooping arms caught his eye. Another, smaller ravine branching down into a nearby box canyon would be to the left, right below it.

The rain was coming down in heavy sheets now, and Lynch made good time. The secondary gully was right where it was supposed to be, and the Air Force colonel quickly outdistanced his pursuers. It was as if he was back in Nam, outracing Charlie through a tropical downpour.

Water cascaded through the maze of ravines, and Lynch found the going much rougher. He lost his footing on the slippery stones several times, and the threat of a flash flood remained on his mind constantly. But the excited voice signals of the security police and the calm verbal commands of their team leader off in the distance spurred him on.

He soon reached the bottom of the hillside and found himself on the flat, muddy floor of a box canyon. The area was all too familiar to Lynch. The sun was hiding behind a wall of dark storm clouds, but the constant sea breeze told him which way was west. He sprinted in the opposite direction, quickly coming to the break in a sheer cliff wall.

Beyond the jutting columns of bluish-green igneous rock, a winding jeep trail rose toward another hilltop, and halfway up the dirt road sat his four-wheel-drive Samuri.

In a few seconds, Lynch had the Suzuki's engine roaring. He executed a sharp U-turn, knowing full well that proceeding in the direction his vehicle was pointed would undoubtedly take him face-to-face with reinforcements, and that speeding back toward the squad of SPs would be just as deadly. Instead Lynch rammed the gearshift into four-wheel drive, left the roadway and raced off down the hillside just as the pursuing security policemen appeared at the box canyon's rocky outlet.

His three pursuers quickly disappeared from view as he barreled straight down a steep, bumpy drop rife with gopher holes and deep pockets of eroded soil.

Several times his head slammed against the roof of the Jeep, despite the fact he'd had the presence of mind to snap his seat belt together when he first turned the ignition key. *Three* blue berets! The thought seemed to strike back at him as a particularly violent bounce slammed his shoulder against the side window. There had been five or six SPs before—now there were only half that number chasing him.

The others had no doubt returned to their own all-terrain vehicle.

No sooner had this second thought entered his head than a dark, Air Force blue pickup, sporting red and blue roof lights and a 50-caliber machine gun mounted in the back, burst forth across the hill directly in front of Lynch. With all four tires off the ground, the vehicle nearly crashed down on top of him.

Lynch brought his Jeep around in a fishtailing slide to the right as the SP driving the pickup fought hard to recover. The colonel headed for a gentle slope between two low hills. He managed to gauge enough of the airmen's progress in his rearview mirror to observe that they tore off their side-mounted radio antenna while plowing through a shoulder-high wall of cacti.

Momentarily he wondered if they'd had time to radio for backup before the mishap, but knew it really didn't matter. The temperature gauge on his dashboard was signaling an overheated motor already. It was only a matter of time before the engine blew.

Lynch roared off between the gentle, rolling slopes and felt a ray of hope flash before him when he saw two low fence lines off in the distance. And beyond them, a meandering, two-laned blacktop highway. If he could make it that far, there might still be a chance he could beat the Air Force patrolmen back to civilization. It would be easier to lose them there, which would give him time to collect his thoughts, plan countermeasures for this unforeseen confrontation, and contact Yuri for advice.

Briefly he wondered if any of the Air Force personnel had recognized him. No one had seen more than the back of his head, so perhaps everything would be okay. If only he could make it through those two sagging fence lines.

Lynch did not think the poorly maintained barbed wire would be able to stop his Jeep—the Samuri was on fairly level terrain now, and quickly gaining speed. He should be able to reach a solid forty miles per hour before impact.

But what the colonel had not planned on was the appearance of a third fence line, partially submerged in the sand. A single metal post, barely visible behind a clump of sagebrush, and rising only a foot and a half above ground, did him in.

He ground his teeth as he felt the oil pan being sheered off. There was a sudden loud clamoring as two rods shot up through the valve cover and thumped repeatedly against the underside of the hood until the motor suddenly died.

Lynch's Jeep did not coast far. Without power to turn the wheels, its speed simply vanished. The front end dipped as linkage and drive shaft seized, and the Samuri, tires entrapped by the salt bed, came to a sluggish halt.

"Keep your hands in plain sight!"

A metallic voice. No squealing tires, no mournful siren. Just a voice, distorted by the SP truck's P.A. system, warning him to behave, and daring him to try something foolish.

In his peripheral vision, Lynch could see why the driver had not bothered to turn on his siren. There was no need:

M-16 barrels bristling from the passenger side window and over the cab's roof were enough to make *any* jackrabbit or coyote yield the right-of-way.

Shrugging his shoulders in resignation, Lynch nudged open the door with his knee and slowly got out of the Jeep. He raised his hands in the air above his head.

1

He had hoped that the dawn jog along Goldenwest Boulevard would remind him of Vietnam, but there simply was no comparison between the sun rising over Orange County's Little Saigon and the swollen, sizzling orb that had always graced the horizons of Indochina.

"It's the tropics," his friend Lyons so often maintained with little if any display of emotion. "There's no sun like the one that warmed your fanny in the tropics, Schwarz. No moon, either, for that matter. No orange crescent moon to light up the battlefield, scare away the rain forest ghosts. The tropics bring everything in close—the moon and the sun, danger and death. You're constantly on the edge of evil in the Orient, guy. And that's what it's all about."

Gadgets Schwarz chuckled silently to himself as he pictured the big ex-cop's lopsided grin. Carl Lyons certainly did have a certain . . . *charm* about him. Yes, that was the word. Charm. Or was it a lack of? The collage of thoughts crowding Schwarz's mind as he sprinted down the deserted avenue forced another laugh to the surface. He missed the team. He actually, genuinely missed them! They were back on the East Coast somewhere—and not likely wasting a second thought on him. But he missed them all the same.

Schwarz was attending a reunion of ex-soldiers at the Orange County Veterans Center some thirty-odd miles south of Los Angeles. It was a meeting of warriors whose skills and attitudes and overall psyche had been forged in Vietnam.

A ten-minute car drive down Harbor Boulevard and the crack counterterrorist expert would be on the Bolsa Strip. Little Saigon. It was the largest resettlement of Vietnamese refugees in the United States. Memory Lane, or Nightmare Alley—he was still not quite sure which.

At first he had experienced no real desire to visit the Strip. Oh, there was that latent curiosity just rippling along the surface, gnawing at him. It made the hairs rise along the back of his neck each time he saw a carload of Asians cruising past. There were more Asians than whites, or even Latinos. *Southeast* Asians. Schwarz could tell; he saw it in their stature and skin tones, in their jet-black hair and ebony eyes. And most of all in their expression. Many of these people had that same thousand-yard stare his old teammates often nursed when they were fresh in from a Lurp recon or free-fire zone. There, life had been a wager, and the odds were against them. Survival was often looked upon as a fluke in the *yin-yang* wheel of destiny. And here in Little Saigon, their faces pressed up against car windows in awe, only the location had changed. Déjà vu, dude.

Schwarz felt no need to confront his Vietnamese experience. There was no healing catharsis awaiting him down on Bolsa. He had already made his peace with the war— in Washington, at the black slash of a monument vets were calling The Wall.

Schwarz had done his time. He'd put in his Tour-365, and then some. Now he was fighting the war on his own terms. And those of Stony Man Farm. Schwarz's days as a counterintelligence advisor in Nam had not been wasted. It had been jungle justice back then. It remained a fragment of that Vietnam vendetta now. Asia's Golden

Triangle had blossomed to consume his precious America. The war had escalated to the home front, and he was in for the duration.

Two women clad in leather shorts and Day-Glo halter tops bicycled past Schwarz. At five feet ten inches and just under a hundred and seventy pounds, his physique was not overly impressive—not in comparison to the top-heavy bodybuilders overpopulating the affluent, white-collar suburbs surrounding Little Saigon—but there was something about his style of running. "Movement without motion" was how Carl Lyons had once described it. Lithe, pantherlike. A cat on two legs.

Schwarz's bronzed face stared into the sun's powerful rays as he ran, and he failed to notice the admiring smiles flashed in his direction by the two female bicyclists. The man's mind was elsewhere. On his muscle tone, and on his past.

Gadgets had not wanted to fly into John Wayne Airport the day before, but he couldn't refuse J.J. Reilly's request. The two grunts had weathered many VC mortar attacks some twenty-odd years earlier, and now J.J. wanted to weather some *ba-muoi-ba*—Vietnamese beer laced with a formaldehyde brew that separated the Boy Scouts from the Kit Carson killers, which was what the double vets called their Arvin trackers back in Void Vicious.

Gold old J.J. Some hundred and ten confirmed kills to his credit, if Gadgets remembered the body count right. J.J. had been a sniper back then in that ethereal world an ocean away. Now he owned a gun shop in Anaheim, only a few blocks from Disneyland, where he sold fiberglass .22 semiautomatic carbines to ex-surfer kids wearing Rambo T-shirts.

J.J. was getting some members of the old MI unit together. Choosing Little Saigon had almost been a joke. Or a dare. Nine of the ten vets showed up, though. The missing man was back in New York. Enduring chemotherapy and his fifteenth hospital stay in half as many years—a bonafide "life member" of the Agent Orange Health Club.

Schwarz stared unblinking into the sun, remembering childhood warnings that doing so would lead to blindness. He also remembered a different, merciless sun that had risen over the Mekong Delta years later, after that same childhood innocence had been snatched away by a doped-up VC sapper's machine gun and the uncompromising realities of hand-to-hand combat.

Nam had been one hell of a rude awakening. It had been after a long night of monsoon rains that he woke to shards of sunlight across his swollen face—fragments of vision that revealed a world of hurt and carnage that had taken place in the dark…the slaughter Schwarz alone had survived.

It was a sight he would never forget—an event he *had* managed to bury in the recesses of his mind. Until this morning, when he stared into a sun that warmed the California coast and would soon rise over Vietnam again.

That so many good men could perish…in so few seconds.

If the sun bathing Little Saigon in bitter crimson evoked memories, it was the fragrance now assaulting his nostrils that took Schwarz right back to Tu Do Street in Sin City's red-light district. Boiling noodles. *Pho.* Vietnamese soup. French bread rolls smothered in hot butter. Steaming sugarcane in plastic baggies. The aroma of ice coffee on the humid, muggy breeze.

Jogging be damned, he thought. He just had to stop.

The soup stall was tucked in between a small Chinese bookshop and a sprawling tape-rental outlet with Vietnam Video emblazoned in neon-blue across its front. It was hidden so far back from the curb that no tourist would ever spot it. But this was Little Saigon. Every Vietnamese refugee in a twenty-block radius knew where the local *pho* soup stall was located. Advertising in Southern California was expensive. In Little Saigon it was unnecessary.

Schwarz glanced back over his left shoulder in preparation for crossing the street, and noticed the dark blue van for the first time. Some sixth sense told him it was following him, even before the driver stepped on the gas pedal.

Gadgets dived to one side, rolling over a number of beat-up trash cans. The van missed him by mere inches.

"My kingdom for Ironman's Colt Python," he muttered under his breath, feeling naked without his own side arm. Actually Schwarz preferred a silenced 93-R, but this morning he'd been in a hurry, abandoning even a backup automatic in its ankle holster, or a half-sheathed commando knife. He'd wanted to get in his morning run before joining the scheduled tour of Reilly's vet center at eight o'clock.

Reacting instinctively, Gadgets grabbed the nearest object that could be used as a weapon—a broom leaning against one of the trash cans. He snapped the bristle section off with a quick heel jab, then—as the van was skidding to a stop several feet away—slammed the shattered end against an iron beam supporting the storefront. More splinters flew.

The van's wheels spun in reverse, producing a blue-gray cloud of burnt rubber and a terrible squealing noise before coming to a stop only inches from him. Gadgets jumped back, and the rear doors flew open.

What appeared to be four Air Force commandos sporting cammies, blue berets and short-barreled Car-15s leaped from the vehicle, their flash suppressors pointed in his face. One barrel already pressed his nose flat.

Gadgets fought the urge to jab out with the jagged broomstick handle. These men were supposed to be on his side. What the hell was going on?

Schwarz's indecision proved his downfall. He was wrestled to the ground and roughly rolled over onto his stomach. Both arms were forced back. Flexicuffs gouged into the flesh along his wrists as someone viciously jerked them shut. "Hey!" he finally yelled at the grim-faced, tight-lipped crew. "I think you clowns got the wrong baby-faced guy."

"Oh, we've got the right no-account diehard!" a husky voice thundered in his ears from behind, as what felt like a cold pistol barrel was positioned against the base of his skull. "Now bend over, sucker, place your head between your knees, and kiss your worthless ass goodbye!"

2

"I'm Lynch, Paul T.," the surrendering suspect said as he stared out at the white salty vastness of Vandenberg Air Force Base's eastern perimeter. He lifted his hands high over his head—palms back, to show they were empty. "Colonel. U.S. Air Force. Serial number 6854..."

His words trailed off with surprise as he slowly turned to find a young woman in her early twenties standing alongside the six male members of the Special Assault Team. She, too, wore olive-drab fatigues below the blue security police beret.

An M-16 was cradled quite casually in her arms—compared to those of her associates—but Lynch was quick to notice her business finger was where it mattered most: on the trigger. The knuckles were white as the rifle's barrel moved to stare him down like a one-eyed bandit. Unyielding. No compromise. Like some jungle wraith riding the midnight trail on a mission of retaliation against those who had lopped off his head. Vietnam vendetta.

"Lace your fingers across the top of your head," ordered a tech sergeant with close-cropped blond hair and thick wrists.

In his peripheral vision, the forty-five-year-old Lynch could see that the SAT members were slowly spreading out—something they should have done initially, his always critical mind chuckled in silence. But perhaps a backup squad manned the ridge line of rocks rising up behind him—he had no way of knowing at this point in the confrontation.

"Do you want me to prone out in the dirt for a felony frisk?" Lynch asked, barely repressing a tight grin, although a nervous tic began working at the edge of his right eye. These hot dogs were obviously not taking any of this lightly.

"No questions!" the female member of the group hissed.

"Just remain where you are, the way you are," the team leader advised. A calm, in-control edge laced his tone now. "And everything will be fine."

Colonel Lynch sensed that he was taller than any member of the assault team. He was not as stocky—he spent most of his free time in the officer's technical library, not the enlisted men's weight room. But height might have its advantages here. And he appeared to be at least twenty years senior to the oldest SP in the group. Experience would also count.

But they were obviously specialists who would not be impressed with his military bearing—the meticulously groomed gray hair and jutting jaw—nor intimidated by the full birds on his shoulders. He could almost hear their thoughts: don't let your rank interfere with our authority, SIR!

The inner laughter subsided as someone took hold of the fingers interlaced atop his head. He felt pressure being applied as he was slowly bent backward, slightly off balance. Powerful, confident hands skilled in the art of quick-frisk rushed across the contours of his frame, probing for weapons.

He concentrated on the woman's words. "You are in a restricted area, sir. We are placing you under apprehension. You will be escorted back to Command and Control Central, where you will be processed in accordance with . . ." She sounded robotic: the words were memorized, issued without one iota of doubt as to their power and authority.

The female SP was several feet behind him now. Lynch sensed that her M-16 was pointed casually at the base of his skull. " . . . and, in accordance with the applicable sections of the uniformed code of military justice, you shall have the right to . . ."

Lynch was hearing only segments of her warning and declaration. It was as if he was being spoken to in a dream, yelled at by an unseen NVA guard while he sleepwalked through the POW camp, headed for the concertina wire and that elusive taste of freedom beyond. " . . . from there you will be transported to . . ."

"Well whatta you know, the guy's packing heat!"

A nagging weight was removed from his left armpit as the Colt .45 was discovered, confiscated and thrown back to one of the other Security Policemen for safekeeping.

The sergeant was removing his wallet, inspecting the credentials. "I'm a colonel," he heard himself saying despite the fog closing in on his mental faculties. "With the Space Command Center in Colorado Springs. You will find authorization orders in my left breast pocket. . . ."

The hand twisting his fingers, pulling at his hair, bending his backbone, suddenly eased. "Colonel *Lynch*?" the team leader questioned, his confident tone cracking somewhat.

"Yes," he sighed, hoping the man did not detect the relief surging in his own voice.

"*The* Colonel Lynch?" one of the other SPs was whispering to another Air Force cop. "*Hawkjaw* Lynch? I wonder if he's the same war hero all the lifers talked about back at San Antonio."

San Antonio. Lynch recognized the reference to the Air Force's law enforcement training school. Had his repu-

tation extended *that* far? Despite the predicament he now
found himself in, such a flattering possibility worked at
inflating his confidence.

"I had no idea, sir," the senior SP said, releasing Lynch
so that he no longer teetered precariously on his heels.
"Well, actually, I *was* warned that you or some other full
bird might be in the area, testing our response times and
such shit, but the Major felt you were still in Colorado at
the NORAD base...."

"We should play this by the book," the female SP
whispered, motioning her fellow team member to the side.
"Cuff his officer ass and escort him back to Command
and Control—full bird or not. Let the duty officer release him."

"Mellow out, Pearce," the senior SP said, dismissing
her cautious behavior with a sneer. "This is *Hawkjaw*
Lynch we're talkin' here. *The* Hawkjaw, girl."

The Air Force colonel slowly turned to confront his
detainers. The sergeant held out Lynch's credentials—
only the slightest misgivings visible in his features as he
silently weighed the situation. The SP knew he had done
the right thing. They had all done their jobs well. But
frisking a full bird at gunpoint? It was a rare opportunity
for a mere sergeant—one to be savored.

"We were briefed that there might be squads of
specially trained intruders attempting to breach security," the female SP said, lowering her rifle. The camouflage jacket failed to hide the smooth contours of her
curves, and suddenly she was female again, not simply
another Blue Beret with an M-16 trained on him. "Navy
Seals, maybe even some clowns from Delta Force...."

"Or possibly some Green Berets from the Army." The
sergeant was talking again as he returned the .45 automatic. His eyes inspected the colonel's own uniform. In
no way did Lynch resemble an intruder. The officer wore

his dress-blue trousers, Class A shirt and Air Force "cunt cap." The latter had been temporarily confiscated by the senior SP while he conducted the cursory body search. And it would have been impossible to miss the white eagles sewn on to the shoulder tabs. The sergeant was slapping the cap against his own thigh now, in a feeble gesture of ridding it of any dirt.

"No problem," Lynch held his hand out. "You people were only doing your job—and doing it quite commendably, I might add." His eyes focused on the tech sergeant's name tag: Tuskin.

"We weren't aware you were in the area, sir," Tuskin said, returning the hat without realizing a handshake was being offered.

"I gave specific orders that word of my arrival and activities not be relayed to the security detachment," Lynch confirmed, brushing off the front of his trousers, even though he had not been spread-eagled in the dirt.

The motion did not escape Sergeant Tuskin. His eyes darted to the ridge line rising around them, and he filed the observation away for future reference. Lynch *had* been proned out. Earlier. Somewhere up in the rocks. Watching. But watching *what*? the senior SP wondered.

"Would you like an escort to the command bunker, sir?" None of the suspicion he was suddenly feeling crept into Tuskin's tone. His conscience kept reminding him that he *admired* this man—this living legend, Hawkjaw Lynch.

"I'll remain in the area, Sergeant, if you don't mind." Lynch produced a warm, brotherly smile that only increased Tuskin's wariness, but nearly disarmed the female SP. Her disposition seemed to change entirely—from skeptic to disciple.

The colonel locked eyes with her, dueled with the woman's mental defenses, brought out an involuntary blush. Feeling a sudden rush of job satisfaction, he turned away, releasing her from the brief trance and the exchange of power. He shifted his concentration to two hawks soaring over the test site in wide, majestic circles.

Tuskin did not miss the exchange. "No, *we* don't mind, Colonel."

"But do you want us to advise the other teams patrolling this sector, sir?" the female SP asked. The colonel glanced at her rank: E-4. And enlisted grade in any foot soldier's army, but a lower rank in the Air Force.

"That won't be necessary." He noted that most of the squad was already returning to its vehicle, which was probably parked several hills away.

Lynch hadn't heard any approaching motors immediately before being intercepted, except the *Specter*'s quad turbines. "There are a few more things I would like to observe in an . . . official capacity, while remaining unobserved," he said, treating Tuskin to a rarely rationed dose of respect—as if he was sharing a privileged little secret with the sergeant. "All for the record, of course: mopping-up operations, post-op security corridors, that sort of thing. You people can carry on. And keep up the good work."

"Of course, sir," the female SP said. Her words seemed to terminate the encounter—her tone outranking even Tuskin for the moment. It was a move the tech sergeant didn't seem to resent. Smiling as if he understood the joke but did not necessarily condone it, he casually slung his M-16, treated Lynch to a semisalute and followed the rest of his team back up through the sand drift and ice plants.

"Good job, Sergeant," Lynch called after him.

Tuskin turned to the female SP matching his powerful stride up the hill. "Official Observer, my ass. That bastard's *up* to something," he muttered.

"He's just doing his job, Tusk," the female SP countered. A few tresses of her long, blond hair had worked their way out from under the confining blue beret. "Don't be so paranoid." She did not reveal that the colonel reminded her of her father. Killed in action, Bien Hoa, RVN. 1972.

Sergeant Tuskin's smile faded. "It's my *job* to be paranoid, *Sergeant* Pearce. I'm telling you, that man's trouble with a capital *T*."

"Then why didn't you place him in custody?" she challenged. "If you've had such a change of heart."

"I'm advising the Major about this incident as soon as we're out of Lynch-The-Great-War-Hero's sight." Tuskin did not seem to recognize the subliminal attitude adjustment.

"Which is exactly what Colonel Lynch would expect you to do. That *both* of you do your job. Shit, Tusk, if he was into the naughty-naughty bit, he sure wouldn't have been wearing his Class A's, complete with name tag. Now would he? If he wasn't legit, you would hardly have gotten to see his ID! You wouldn't have coaxed word one from the man. He spent five years in a North Vietnamese POW camp, you know. Hell, we never would have *found* him, probably. And if we had, he'd probably have responded with a hollowpoint to your head instead of that handshake back there."

The wry smile returned to Tuskin's face. "I love it when you curse in uniform, Sergeant Pearce." She had moved ahead of him on the steep trail, and he lightly patted her behind.

Pearce halted midway up the hillside, whirled and tried to slap him, but Tuskin caught the flying, openhanded chop while it was still airborne. "You forgot who *taught* you that move." His grin grew nearly ear-to-ear as he checked the progress of the rest of the team. They were over the hill now—out of sight and out of mind.

Pearce countered with a backward kick to the groin, but Tuskin pivoted at the last moment, taking the brunt of the impact on his thigh. It barely phased him, but Pearce's retort seemed to cut deep. "And I don't *fool around* on duty, *Sergeant*!" Her whisper was harsh and to the point. "Save the grab-ass for your boyfriends back in the barracks, okay?"

Tuskin's smile dropped. As he watched Pearce's firm haunches negotiate the thorn bushes now crowding the trail up ahead, and envisioned the after-duty embrace that would see the two of them locked together in tangled limbs on some sand dune beneath the desert moon, he all but forgot about Colonel Paul Lynch and the incident on the rocky crag below.

3

Tucking his head between his knees, Gadgets Schwarz instantly recognized J.J. Reilly's drill instructor tone. But he still could not see the stocky man.

Reilly punched Schwarz hard enough on the shoulder to start a bruise rising. "You're the no-account diehard who went *AWOL* on us last night," he accused. "The low-life rat fink who failed to report to our clandestine party on the pier."

"J.J.!" Schwarz squealed as he was hoisted off the ground and carried toward the van. A jump boot bounced off his nose. "Is this an *official* wing nut operation, sanctioned by the U.S. Air Farce, or what? This is overdoing it a little bit, don't you think—even for the notorious Raunchy Reilly!"

"Silence maggot!" J.J. commanded, jabbing him in the side with a military swagger stick this time.

"J.J., I surrender, man!" Gadgets could not stop laughing now as someone started tickling his other side with a jump boot sporting a mirror-quality finish. He could see the fuzzy reflection of his own face in the airman's spit-shined toe. "Enough is enough! I surrender! But I've got a good reason for—"

"No excuses!" Reilly's baritone voice boomed in his ears. "Excuses are for draft dodgers, slick!"

"Not an excuse! A *reason*!" Schwarz pleaded good-naturedly as the airmen paused at the van's open rear doors and began swinging him back and forth in preparation for the toss. "I had to sleep off the jet lag, man! Just got in from Chieng Mai and a thirteen-hour time change!"

"One...two..." They chanted with each increasingly powerful swing, ignoring Schwarz's pleas.

"Sure!" Reilly taunted as Gadgets caught sight of the three scantily-clad women sitting inside the dark van. "And since when has an R & R to Thailand kept you from being the lowlife of the party?" J.J. demanded.

"But really, Reilly!" Gadgets protested. "I was only—"

"Well, it just so happens we voted to bring the floor show to *you*, Gadgets!"

The women pounced on Schwarz as soon as he skidded face-first across the metal floor of the van. The rear doors slammed shut, and he was enveloped in darkness and warm flesh as the vehicle's rear tires began spinning once more.

"Don't I even get to take the handcuffs off?" he screamed after his vet buddy as the van roared off toward the Bolsa Strip, headed for the heart of Little Saigon.

Raunchy Reilly simply laughed.

WHEN THE VAN pulled into a back alley in the heart of Little Saigon five minutes later, Schwarz expected to be released and treated to some sort of semipleasant surprise. But when the van's rear doors finally did open, no one, including the women, made a move to release him. Instead two familiar faces glanced into the vehicle's dark interior.

A stocky blond male, sporting grim features and a squared-off jaw, shook his head in the affirmative. "That's him!" he said, nodding directly at Gadgets, who in turn grinned back in mock appreciation of the new-comer's loud sports coat. "That's the scumbag!"

The big man with the lineman's physique stood in at roughly six foot two and a solid one hundred and ninety pounds and had, in fact, played a little college football twenty or so years earlier at Cal State. His stare—a bleak, icy gray-blue with the endless coldness of a barren glacier—drilled into Schwarz with no hint of controlled comradery.

"You've got the right schmuck!" a snarling Latino standing beside the first man acknowledged. He was about three inches shorter and fifteen pounds lighter than the blonde, but with no less determination in his jet-black eyes. Once a dark brown, his hair was now wavy white and combed back—not bleached by too many years beneath some tropical sun, but discolored after more than his share of bloody Asian battlefields and the Stateside slaughters that had followed.

Gadgets did not seem worried about either of the two, however. "Ironman!" he called out to the unsmiling blonde. His eyes shifted to the man in banker's gray. "Pol! What are *you* two clowns doing here?"

He was staring at the rest of Able Team—the duo he had thought was back in Virginia's Shenandoah Valley, at their Blue Ridge Mountain retreat, pumping iron in Stony Man Farm's new gymnasium. They were the two crack, antiterrorist experts he'd been musing about only an hour earlier: Carl "Ironman" Lyons and Rosario "Politician" Blancanales. "Tell these jerks and jerkettes they got the wrong dude, guys!" he demanded.

Schwarz was expecting instant recognition—immediate assistance. Instead he received total indifference. "Dude?" The grim-faced blonde cocked an eyebrow at Gadgets, then turned to one of the Air Policemen. "Yeah, you *definitely* got the right ace. Now take him to the hellhole for a little round of truth or consequences!" Carl Lyons was slapping a lead sap against the palm of his hand as anticipation gleamed in his narrowed eyes. "And save a little meat for me!"

"But Ironman . . ." Schwarz resumed his protests, only to have the van's rear doors slam shut in his face again.

The girl on his left wrapped her arm around his throat, pulling him back slightly, off balance. He felt his head bounce off the metal wall of the van and, for a moment, stars swirled in front of his eyes.

"This is ridiculous," he muttered under his breath. His situation was fast progressing past the limits of any practical joke. And what the hell were Pol and Ironman doing in Southern California, anyway? Had some sudden mission necessitated their immediate arrival to Orange County?

Flashbacks of a TV news story he'd watched only an hour earlier—before starting out on his job—returned to haunt the electronics wizard. The segment had been about a KGB double agent exposed recently by the CIA in Washington, D.C. The Kremlin had sent out an assassination team to bring the operative home. In a box.

And they had been deadly efficient.

Former comrades of the spy had no doubt been ordered to terminate him. Gadgets nodded in agreement with his swirling thoughts. Was he now finding himself in a similar set of dead-end circumstances? Had some insane happenings at Stony Man Farm transpired in his absence? Was there some misunderstanding here? Had some old enemy, bent on revenge, set him up? It had happened before—and to less enlightened masters of dirty tricks and doublespeak than himself. Had some low-life denizen from Schwarz's past surfaced to wreak vengeance on the counterterrorist—even going to the successful extent of deceiving Lyons and Blancanales and Brognola?

Had the Chief himself put out the hit?

Conflicting emotions seized the veteran's usually calm demeanor. His routine Socratic method of solving unexpected problems by framing inner thoughts as questions abandoned him now, and Schwarz felt the hairs along the nape of his neck bristle anxiously.

Panic was setting in, lacing the maddening collage of possibilities filling his head. Schwarz was well aware that Fate might have finally dealt him an unfair hand—his colleagues could very possibly have been transformed into his enemies. Just like that. It was how espionage and the cloak-and-dagger game were played. And there were no second place winners in this contest.

Should the tables be turned, and if one of the others were targeted for termination, Gadgets knew he would have to grind his teeth and proceed with getting the job done.

It was why he'd made so few friends in Vietnam. Death was too freely dealt in the Orient. Better to just be a part of a well-oiled killing machine, leaving all emotions out of it—casting all friendships aside. Until after the war. Until after your Tour-365 was completed and that gut-wrenching sound of your freedom bird's wheels lifting free of Tan Son Nhut Airport's runway finally reached your relieved ears.

Yes, that had to be it. Someone at Puzzle Palace or Disneyland Central—perhaps even Stony Man Farm—had put out the word: issue Hermann Schwarz's one-way ticket to oblivion. Pol and Ironman were no longer associates. They were the enforcers coming to get him. And they'd do their job coldly, efficiently, if the facts were sufficiently stacked against Gadgets, if some brilliant unseen enemy on the other side of the bamboo wall had constructed his scam cleverly enough.

But no! This could not be happening! The three of them *were* more than just a finely tuned squad of weapons experts and counterterrorists. Over the years, they had become more than just the President's Able Team. They'd become friends as well.

Surely Carl and Rosario would see through this! Surely they would detect any bogus con game manufactured by those cold, calculating enemies that lurked in the shadows. But there had certainly been less important misunderstandings that had eventually led to bigger catastrophes on the planet. Why should *he* be so blessed as to escape the cruel winds of destiny?

But Gadgets Schwarz—guerrilla warfare expert and technological Apache extraordinaire—did not have long to ponder all these nerve-wracking developments. The van lurched to a sudden stop.

He heard the engine sputter, cough, then putter again as the driver removed the ignition key and the vehicle refused to die without a fight. "Give 'em hell, pal," Gadgets muttered under his breath. "Stay hard and—"

"Shut up!" One of the women elbowed him in the side, but not hard enough to do any damage. He doubted the jab would even leave a bruise—not like the one Reilly had inflicted, in any event. A good sign? Schwarz thought not. Something was up. And he'd rather take all they could dish out than have to worry about pulled punches and ulterior motives.

A trio of sirens burst forth outside the truck's walls, and this definitely raised Schwarz's spirits. Were they being pulled over by a police officer? Perhaps he had a chance at straightening this whole mess out before it was too late. Before the wing nuts in the front seat delivered him to some roadside gully's shallow grave on the edge of town.

Then, more sirens. An entire chorus of them, encircling the van. *Salvation!* Schwarz felt a wave of relief flood him. Perhaps he'd be able to talk his way out of this snafu after all.

The rear doors flew open again, and it became immediately evident that he was in the restricted-access parking lot of a police department: black-and-white cruisers were parked everywhere, three and four rows deep. Uniformed patrolmen were getting in or out of half of them, loading equipment into trucks, inspecting emergency equipment or simply gathering beside certain of the units to chat. Schwarz nodded at the realization: it was obviously shift change at the local P.D.

His eyes scanned side doors, focusing on the nearest official emblem. Below the City of Westminster seal was emblazoned the caption: *To Serve and Protect*. On more than a few rear bumpers, red-and-black stickers proclaimed: *World-class Protection*—an obvious throwback to the '84 Summer Olympics, which had been held in Los Angeles.

Schwarz also spotted a familiar vehicle parked between two K-9 dog team units: a bronze-toned Plymouth Grand Voyager minivan. It looked exactly like the van Hal Brognola had been praising up and down back at Stony Man. In addition to refinements under the hood, the Voyager could be equipped with an interior computer system and detachable inner paneling that would allow for the secret storage of weapons in molded recesses. The presence of the van seemed highly coincidental.

It both relieved and worried Gadgets. The Chief could be the key to his partners' clowning. Or he could be the catalyst behind the ordered demise of one Hermann Schwarz.

His view of the mobile command post was suddenly obscured when Ironman's massive wrists reached in to grab him. Schwarz felt himself lifted up off the van's metal floorboards and carried out into harsh sunlight that temporarily blinded him.

Lyons flipped Schwarz over his shoulder and carried him down a gently sloping concrete drive that dropped beneath the multistoried police headquarters into an underground garage.

Shadows enveloped them again, and once Schwarz's eyes adjusted to his dimly lighted surroundings, he realized dozens of officers were backing off, staring at the five Air Force policemen escorting the plainclothes duo and their prisoner to a security elevator.

No one challenged them. Lyons obviously still looked like an undercover cop to another badge. Blancanales had that authoritative gait and cynical expression down pat as well. Gadgets hoped they were perplexed by his own presence and would ask about the captive, but no such luck.

"Been hunting?" one patrolman asked. That was all Gadgets rated, it seemed—wisecracks from a flatfoot.

"And the woods were full of weirdos today," Ironman grunted as the assemblage squeezed into the elevator and its doors clamped shut, sealing them inside a granite shaft. The car began rising.

"Still on the fourth floor?" Blancanales asked one of the blue-bereted security policemen.

"Right," a young, nineteen-year-old with close-cropped black hair and wire-rim glasses responded without emotion. "They've taken out a couple walls recently. It's a much bigger briefing room now."

Briefing room? Schwarz's eyebrows came together. He'd thought they were taking him to Interrogation. What the—

"Think he's had enough?" Blancanales asked, suddenly turning to Carl Lyons.

"Probably." Ironman allowed himself a tight grin. "But I haven't. I could continue with this farce the rest of the week."

"Yeah, I hear where you're coming from, brother." Pol's chuckle was one he was obviously savoring. "But we'd probably better play it cool and professional. Don't want Westminster's finest to think we're a bunch of bozos. Better free the freeloader."

"Why you guys—" Schwarz's confidence returned to him instantly. His chest expanded as he mentally formulated the appropriate protest, but before he could continue with any verbal assault, Lyons was releasing his hold on the electronics wizard and dumping him onto the floor of the elevator.

Rising into an Asian-style squat with his hands still bound behind his back, Schwarz's exclamation was cut short as the elevator lurched to a stop, its doors slid open and he found his nose level with a set of smooth knees. Black fishnet stockings camouflaged the knees somewhat. They belonged to a pair of long, tanned legs that seemed to rise endlessly toward the hem of a bright purple miniskirt.

Schwarz glanced up beyond the shapely figure that continued above the legs, and into the eyes of a green-eyed redhead. *Hooker.* His mind popped forth the word, but his eyes dropped again—to the gold badge hanging on the undercover decoy's black plastic belt. "Looking for something?" the female detective asked, legs shifting almost provocatively as she rested one hand on her hip, waiting for a reply. There was the slightest hint of intrigue gleaming in her eyes as she appraised the three strangers' rock-hard physiques.

Blushing, Gadgets turned on his haunches slightly, bringing the handcuffed wrists into view. "Could you spare a key?'' he asked sheepishly, forgetting that flexi-cuffs required wire cutters.

The investigator's eyes locked on to Carl Lyons, who was already fishing through front pockets for his snips.

''In-service training,'' Blancanales offered as an explanation to the redhead. ''It kind of got out of hand.''

''Obviously,'' the female detective said, pursing her lips as she cast Schwarz a ''poor little boy'' frown, then stepped into the elevator just before the doors slid shut again.

''About time you clowns showed up!''

Hal Brognola appeared inside a nearby doorway. ''I'm nursing my fourth cup of P.D. issue brew,'' he said. ''And the last thing I need right now is a caffeine overdose.''

The sight of the older man's Honduran cigar brought a flood of relief through Gadget Schwarz's system. ''These guys decked my butt, Chief!'' Schwarz feigned an odd mixture of pain and betrayal.

Brognola read loss of face, but ignored his guerrilla warfare expert's expression. ''Come on, come on, you guys!'' He turned his back on the trio and disappeared inside the cavernous briefing room. ''We got business to attend to.''

''Patience, Chief.'' Blancanales smiled, but Brognola didn't seem to notice.

''Places to go,'' Lyons muttered as he strode from the elevator. ''Things to see,...'' He grabbed Schwarz's wrist to help him to his feet. '' 'Patience,' he says....''

''Patience my ass.'' Schwarz jerked his wrists away as the ex-policeman finally removed the fiberglass handcuffs. ''I'm in the mood to *kill* something.''

4

Paul Lynch cupped a hand to his ear until he heard the roar of twin gun-jeep engines. He remained crouched beside the ridge line's crevice, using its natural acoustics to amplify all noise penetrating the canyon, until the sound of a third souped-up motor—the one belonging to the SAT truck—also faded. The Alert Team was leaving the area, heading west. Back toward the command point.

He knew that they would report the encounter to their commanding officer, and that there would be additional patrols saturating the area. Even now, after the *Specter*'s mock landing mission was completed.

The colonel wiped a gritty film of sweat from his forehead. A layer of dead gnats and mosquitoes came away with it, but the pests following him through the blanket of heat that smothered the desert floor were the least of his problems. Lynch sighed with relief—at least Sergeant Tuskin had not radioed for his immediate supervisor to respond to the scene, or even requested instructions from his superior. *That* could have complicated matters. Instead he had made an on-the-spot field decision based on the facts at hand and what he already knew about the colonel. And for that error in judgment, Lynch was grateful.

He hardly noticed the rattlesnake coiled off to one side, shaking its tail at him in frantic warning as he moved deeper into concealment among the scrub oak and cacti.

Rather than striking, however, the snake slithered off into the underbrush, irritated but in no mood for confrontation. Perhaps it sensed the rain approaching again and desired a hasty return to shelter. Storm clouds passed by low overhead now.

Soon, sheets of water danced across the land in furious, marauding attacks. They beat down on Lynch, plastering his neatly trimmed hair against his skull.

The dry stretch of salt and sand was fast becoming a muddy quagmire on either side of the packed-earth or concrete runways, and he was already soaked. But he knew that the rain would put a damper on security operations taking place on the lake bed below. The various Air Force squads would rush to check their respective quadrants of responsibility, secure the perimeter, then settle in for the night.

The USS *Specter* would sit in the middle of its vast security corridor, surrounded by elite teams of counterterrorist and antisabotage security police. But once again his credentials would get him through the roadblocks and checkpoints. And allow him to inspect the *Specter*—run NORAD-sanctioned "tests" on the advanced components of her military hardware compartment.

Although the *Specter* was a mock-up of the actual space shuttle, its cargo section was not. The same equipment that NASA was hoping to send up with the next orbital mission was now in place and operable—the rumbling guts of *Specter*.

Lynch did not wait for the heavy rainfall to subside. He climbed the slippery cliff face to a point where he could scan the surrounding terrain and verify that no other security teams were canvassing the area, or that Sergeant Tuskin had surreptitiously returned to monitor his activities.

Then the colonel descended to a shallow crevice marked on the field map that had been left in his safety deposit box by his Soviet contact, the mystery man known to him as Yuri the Ogre. The camouflaged shaft was right where the map indicated it would be.

Lynch removed the intricate layers of packed mud, wire mesh and finally, wooden beams. Inside the six-foot pit was an aluminum container measuring roughly one meter square and sealed with wire tape. An encoding device equipped with a transmitter was attached to one of the outer seals. So Yuri will know that I have reached this point in the mission, Lynch nodded sadly.

The senior Air Force veteran did not enjoy assuming the role of traitor to his homeland. But none of this could be helped. In the end, he hoped mankind would judge him with some semblance of compassion. If mankind survived.

Faint visions of Xuan, suffering back in some Vietnamese hellhole, passed in front of his mind's eye— like fluttering frames of a motion picture—and the guilt enveloped him. As it always did.

He shook his head violently, trying to end the flashback, and found the images were replaced by the female air cop's young face—her innocent, schoolgirl's eyes twenty years younger than Xuan's. He recalled the unexpected desire he had felt for the shapely SP, and a wave of shame rolled in like high surf at twilight, bringing with it an even sharper likeness of Xuan. As he tapped at the envelope taped to the small of his back—the envelope stuffed with hundred dollar bills that the otherwise meticulous SP had failed to detect during the body frisk— Lynch remembered that it was because of the woman imprisoned in Vietnam that he had become involved in this operation.

After pitching a poncho liner overhead to shield the box and much of the crevice from the elements, Lynch removed the heavy bolt cutters taped to the outside of the container and began removing the device's protective covering.

Within fifteen minutes he had removed and adjusted the satellite relay switching device. Oddly the rainstorm passed with the same abruptness in which it had arrived, and Lynch was actually disappointed with the ease in which the mission was proceeding. He climbed out of the crevice with the Kremlin-sanctioned and KGB-made equipment strapped into a rucksack on his back.

Once back on the ridge line, Lynch made his way toward the cliff's edge, wasting no time to take in the series of rainbows and purple downpours marking the storm's distant border. He quickly located the steep footpath, and proceeded to a narrow ledge twenty or so feet down the cliff's sheer face.

There he located another opening chiseled into the soft clay. If only the Air Force had intercepted the team of agents who initiated this whole scheme, his mind screamed. I wouldn't be here now, digging my own grave deeper. But there was no choice in the matter. Not now. It was too late.

Lynch extended the switching device's tripodlike legs. Anchoring bolts were already in place; he merely had to screw the iron legs into the buried base plate, then attach the primary device itself, a platinumlike sphere that was eighteen inches in diameter.

A few minutes later he tugged at the contraption, shifting his weight, trying to dislodge it from several different angles, using all manner of force. Subliminally perhaps, he almost wanted the switching device to break free and tumble down the cliff wall into the maze of jagged sedimentary rocks piled a hundred feet blow. But it refused to budge. As usual, the colonel had attacked his mission with a head-on determination that did not allow for failure.

Lynch removed the Velcro straps of a black felt cover, instantly cowering against a nearby outcropping of shale at the unexpected noise. But there was no one around to hear the harsh rasp of peeling Velcro. His pace increased dramatically now that this phase of the mission was almost over.

Lynch fed a series of numbers into a glowing combination lock, and a metal base plate popped open, revealing the programming panel. He removed a tiny strip of microfilm from beneath the emblem that was pinned to his cap, and which indicated his rank.

Whoever programmed Skylink had the option of manually typing in the necessary coordinates and solar reference points. But Lynch chose to simply feed the microfilm into a secondary input slot, loading the system automatically. He was nervous, and any mistakes at this stage of the game would result in a tragic series of catastrophic events. Or so the Ogre had warned. And Lynch already had enough guilt nagging at his conscience.

A barely audible series of seven beeps told him the system was now operable and on-line. He typed in a three-digit code that Yuri had given him, and received the appropriate response.

A sudden screeching overhead forced Lynch back against the cliff wall. But it was only a startled hawk that appeared, flapping its wings a few feet in front of his face. He drew his pistol but the big bird quickly vanished, dropping to the lake bed below before ascending into a steep climb along the cliff walls and soaring out over the landing site.

Sighing loudly as he listened to his excited heart thump against his rib cage, Lynch holstered the .45, typed in another challenge, then a third, and after receiving the proper answer to both, flipped the transmit switch.

He immediately received a blue go light.

Without hesitating, he shut down the power system and fed a ten-digit code into Skylink's complex timer. As a predetermined military timetable approached, the relay switching device would lock on to a NORAD satellite already in orbit and reactivate Skylink. It would awake, humming atop its monsterlike tripods, ready to send radio commands to the space shuttle as it passed above.

Now, aside from gaining access to *Specter*'s sophisticated bowels and running a test scan of the mock shuttle's computer system, there was nothing more for the Air Force colonel to do except await the KGB agent's next directive. He knew that the next mission would take him back to the desolate Air Force base during the upcoming space shuttle launch—he would be required to feed several critical operational directives into the ship's computer banks.

They would be directives that would cause the space shuttle's shipboard computers to anticipate and/or supersede any commands from the President should Air Force One be destroyed.

Beyond that, Lynch knew nothing of the Soviets' plans. Yuri was adamant that Lynch had no *need* to know further details of the clandestine mission. It indicated a lack of trust, and for some reason, the Russian's attitude cut deeply.

Damn the planners, an inner voice protested. Why did those in charge at NASA decided to build a West Coast launchpad at Vandenberg in the first place?

He knew all the answers, of course. There were usually better weather conditions in Southern California than at Florida's Cape Canaveral. Launch facilities on the West Coast would alleviate the problems associated with ferrying space shuttles back to the Kennedy Space Center after they had landed on the West Coast. And shifting many of the space shuttle projects to Vandenberg would effectively block the Cuban eavesdropping network out of Havana.

The USS *Atlantis* was already warehoused in California, and the *Enterprise*—which had been ear-marked to become a permanent display at the Smithsonian Institute—was recommissioned into active service and at that very moment was being loaded onto a 747 jumbo jet for the relay ride to Vandenberg.

Colonel Paul Lynch climbed back to the cliff's edge, then made his way to the ridge line. He crossed several hilltops dense with prickly, uniform-ripping foliage, until he once again overlooked the USS *Specter*. It was time for the next phase of the mission.

The skies had turned black with warning. There was a tempest brewing in the distance, over the eastern hori-zon, and rushing toward him. Cumulus clouds billowed overhead already.

Lynch noted that the rainbows were nowhere to be seen.

5

More than fifty uniformed law enforcement officers sat behind connecting tabletops in the brightly lighted briefing room. Interspersed among their civilian ranks were a number of Air Force Security Policemen wearing green fatigues and blue berets. M-16s leaned precariously against thighs or the edges of tabletops. Gadgets Schwarz recognized a Vandenberg SAT patch on one airman near the front of the room—an officer, wearing captain's bars as well.

Hal Brognola, Stony Man Farm's chief of operations and liaison with the U.S. Justice Department, stood at the back of the giant room. Arms folded across his chest as he leaned against the wood paneling and chewed on his ever-present Honduran cigar, the big man watched a grizzled old desk sergeant conduct the final, wind-down phases of a relief-shift briefing.

Only a few heads had turned when Able Team had entered. Most of the policemen had either been engrossed by something the roll call sergeant was saying, or simply intrigued by the presence of the teenaged SPs whose routine service weapons actually consisted of automatic rifles with thirty-round banana clips curling forward from their ammo wells.

"So, that's it!" The sergeant in charge of the briefing slapped the side of his podium. "Let's saddle up and hit the bricks. Make a point of saturating the shopping plazas along Brookhurst Avenue and the Bolsa Strip. Auto-theft Bureau has advised me that the little asshole Viet gang-bangers are heavy into Toyota Celicas this week. Let's see if we can curb this month's GTA stats a little, okay, gentlemen?" He seemed to spot an irritated frown lingering in his peripheral vision, and the sergeant's eyes rolled toward the ceiling. "*And* ladies..." he finally added. "I want to see field interrogation contact cards on any street hoodlum who so much as spits on the side-walk, is that understood?"

A general groan of discontent filled the briefing room as the Westminster patrol officers began filing out into a crowded access hallway. The SPs remained seated, how-ever.

Schwarz watched a few of the officers stop to confer with the Air Force policemen regarding their M-16s. Here and there, barrels rose toward the ceiling as ex-SPs, Nam vets and a few weekend warriors in the group examined hand guards and flash suppressors, taking a nostalgic cruise down memory lane before heading out to their pa-trol units and the cruel reality that was Orange County's Little Saigon.

"Thanks for letting us sit in, sir," Brognola overheard the Air Force captain stating his appreciation to the briefing sergeant.

"No sweat, despite the ultrashort notice." The re-sponse was a hearty one. "Wish you guys would level with me about what brings you to town, however. You're sure as shit not interested in hot cars cruisin' the Bolsa Strip."

Hal Brognola entered the conversation—a chilly wind swirling through a forest clearing. "Got a briefing my-self that needs to be given." His hand swept the room to encompass both the Air Force security policemen and the three newcomers in civilian attire. "Your P.D. was the closest 'secure station' where I'd have access to a CAD information system and slide projector facilities.''

"Well, we've certainly got everything you'd need for a slide show. One of our guys just got back from three weeks in Tahiti and truly has some juicy shots to show his boys on night watch. But I didn't know we had a caddy system or whatever you just now called it—''

"CAD," Brognola repeated with a smile. "Computer-Aided Dispatch system."

"Oh, *that* piece of shit." The sergeant's smile broadened. "Is that what they call it—Caddy? Well, it's down half the time for repairs, pal. The guys hate it—allows the dispatchers to keep more of an eye on their activities out on the street. When it's up, that is," the sergeant revealed with a wry wink. "If you catch my meaning...."

"I think I do," Brognola nodded. "But it's not the dispatch segment of the system we need to access. CAD can also connect with sophisticated information banks across the country. That feature was primarily designed to better incorporate data available from NCIC and Department of Justice computer banks, but its developers realized the system could also be altered to accommodate programs in other law enforcement and criminal justice fields such as research and statistics. But, basically, with the right access codes in hand, the system can gain entry into just about any information bank open to other government agencies."

"Something tells me you're talking *military* information banks," the police sergeant said, glancing at the nearby captain's blue beret for emphasis.

NASA's streamlined space emblem flashed through Brognola's mind just then, but he did not correct the sergeant's guess. "Something like that," he agreed. His grin flattened out, but the twinkle in his eye remained.

"This thing really has the authority of the President behind it—like my patrol commander was telling me?"

"Yes," Brognola said solemnly, "it does."

"Top Gun himself," Carl Lyons added as he moved beside Brognola.

"Well, I wish you G-man types would level with a lowly desk sergeant. Just once, for a change. I half expect to see James Bond come through that door next," he motioned toward the entryway.

"Bond's British," Pol Blancanales chuckled. "We're red, white and blue, through and through. And better."

"Well...." But the police sergeant was already walking away.

As if they were familiar with the layout of the building and had used the briefing room before, two young SPs appeared at a side door. They were wheeling in a slide projector.

Gadgets Schwarz, still rubbing at the flexicuff abrasions on his wrists, listened to the only sound in the room—the projector table's wheels squeaking.

Then there came an odd buzzing sound, and Carl Lyons turned to watch a large film screen slowly drop from the ceiling. Never had anything that fancy at the LAPD, he thought.

From a briefcase he had carried into the building, Brognola removed a circular slide carrier and gently placed it on top of the projector. He glanced around the room, counted about twenty Air Force SPs in attendance, took in a deep breath, and lifted the microphone from the podium.

Brognola wasn't used to briefing so many people. He preferred small numbers—like the elite commandos making up Able Team or Phoenix Force—but, as usual, the President was calling the shots on this one, and the Commander In Chief wanted Air Force involvement without debate. Under the circumstances, Brognola reluctantly had to agree with the man's strategy.

Carl Lyons dimmed the lights, and as the room began to darken, Brognola noticed a shadow lurking near the back of the room. An unmoving shadow with an odd, silvery glow where a silhouette target's bull's-eye might be—right over the heart. It was the police briefing sergeant, the two-legged grizzly in P.D. blue.

"Can we, uh, help you, Sarge?" Blancanales had also spotted the badge sparkle out of the corner of one eye.

"Naw...got some time to kill...just thought I'd sit in on *your* briefing."

"I'm afraid that's not possible." Brognola's tone was no longer cordial.

"What?" Even at this distance and in the darkness, Brognola could see that the sergeant's eyes were scanning the much younger faces of the silent SPs. His expression said that his no-nonsense years of street experience overshadowed their year or two in a fancy blue beret.

"It's classified, Sarge. No offense," Brognola said, sounding friendly again. "Chickenshit GI Joe games, you know?"

Pol Blancanales smiled. Such a politician, he was thinking.

"No offense," Brognola repeated.

"And none taken." A smile returned to the sergeant's grim countenance. But once again his unamused vulture's eyes scanned the youthful faces of the SPs, and he grunted before leaving the room.

"Police politics," Lyons said, moving beside Blancanales. "Such a pain in the ass."

As the room became completely dark and a bright beam of light splashed forth from the projector, Brognola replaced the microphone and moved closer to his three men, addressing them first. "You fell victim to a—how should

I phrase it?—a kidnapping this morning." His eyes locked onto Schwarz's, then shifted to Ironman's. "How did Gadgets react?"

Lyons released a tense chuckle. "I thought he was going to shit a brick, Chief. Then, after it was all over, *kill* us."

"And slowly." Blancanales grinned as well, but Brognola's face remained creased in a deep frown.

"I'm not interested in the aftermath," he said glancing back at Schwarz again. "How did you feel when you were being hustled off the street, into the Air Force van."

Gadget's face grew solemn as well. "I wasn't sure *what* to think."

"Give it your best shot," Brognola said sarcastically.

"Well, on the one hand I was definitely being accosted by strangers, although I *did* recognize a voice in the crowd afterward. But when the hijack first went down, I was really experiencing mixed signals, Boss."

"Mixed signals?" Brognola cocked an eyebrow in skeptical response.

"Sure. My gut instincts told me to kick ass and fight for my life. But these guys were…friendly forces. They were wearing blue berets—air cops! And driving what appeared to be a genuine Air Force issue van."

"And later?" Brognola pressed.

"Later?" The lines at the edges of Schwarz's eyes deepened. Had there been a "later?" All he could remember was the roust, then arriving at this police station.

"When Carl and Pol showed their lovely faces, but took the side of the goons in blue—abandoning you to the bad guys, so to speak. Ignoring you," Brognola specified. "Treating you suddenly like just so much shit—and after so many years of…brotherhood. How did you feel? What was your gut telling you?"

Gadgets swallowed hard before answering. Was he being set up to be the brunt of some insane joke? What was the purpose of all this? When was it going to end? "My gut was twisted in knots," he said finally. "Half of me wanted to wake up from the nightmare. But the other half knew that the situation could be real. That—even if I was the object of some horrible mistake—my destiny of doom might have finally found its way to my doorstep. After all, we're not Boy Scouts here. This ain't no field trip. The game's for keeps.

"In my heart I knew it was very possible that a mistake had been made somewhere—that a bogus hit had been put out on me. That somewhere down the line the error would be realized but, by that time, it would be too late. Yours truly would be terminated, ticket cancelled. These two clowns—" he motioned to his longtime partners "—would do their job. And then they'd feel like shit afterward, but—"

"We'd get over it," Carl Lyons said, flashing his teeth brightly. The grin reminded Gadgets of a bright ivory crescent moon hanging low over the tropics.

"I'm sure you would," Brognola sighed. Now he allowed himself a smile as well. "Okay," he said, "so much for today's lesson. You claimed earlier that you experienced mixed feelings. That description may prove to be what this upcoming mission will be all about. You'll be working with men and women whose integrity you'd ordinarily never doubt. I'm talking American military people—Air Force security police personnel."

"I don't get the connection," Schwarz said, although he feared Brognola's remarks were clear as crystal, and this pained him as he glanced over at J.J. Reilly. Reilly sat on the other side of the room in a group of older SPs, chatting quietly among themselves as they waited for the slide show and briefing to begin.

"Expect mixed signals from here on out." He lowered his voice so that he was sure only the three members of Able Team could hear him. "Trust no one—I don't care how patriotic to the country or dedicated to the job they sound or seem. I've had my misgivings from the onset, but the closest Delta Force platoons are in the Philippines, ensuring there's no breach of security at our Air Force and Naval bases there following all the recent NPA-inspired unrest...."

"The Filipino communist party?" Schwarz asked, cocking an eyebrow.

"Right. They call themselves the 'New People's Army,' to be precise. Anyway, half our other counterterrorist units are being shuffled around, and the President wants us in on this one in hopes that the press corps doesn't get a whiff of spilt blood."

"And just what exactly do you mean by 'this one,' Chief?" Blancanales asked crossing his eyes in a feeble attempt to force Schwarz to crack a grin.

"There are possibly one or more traitors operating at NASA's new launch facility at Vandenberg Air Force Base," Brognola said, remaining unsmiling as well. "It will be our job to detect and neutralize the intruders that Mission Control expects will attempt to threaten the upcoming West Coast space shuttle launch this month. The Pentagon is not sure if the threat being posed comes from outside the facility or within."

"What?" Carl Lyons looked suddenly sad as he read between Brognola's words.

"We'll be infiltrating a security police squadron at Vandenberg," Hal Brognola said without emotion.

6

The security guard motioned for other SPs at the static post to join him the moment he spotted the tall figure walking up the middle of the road.

Colonel Paul Lynch was careful to keep his hands a few inches out from his sides as he approached the test site checkpoint—to ensure that the sentries could see he was not carrying a weapon. The Air Force officer had disposed of his Colt .45 pistol, secreting it inside one of the containers that had earlier housed the Skylink device.

The SPs lowered their guard as Lynch entered the sphere of brilliant floodlights arcing out from the guard shack. The beam from one of their powerful flashlights bounced off the eagle emblem attached to the front left edge of Lynch's cap.

"Evening, Colonel," the ranking SP said, producing a salute that would represent the men standing casually behind him as well.

"Lynch, Paul T." He returned the salute smartly, an ID card already in his outstretched hand, a friendly smile across his dust-caked features. "I believe you're expecting me, gentlemen. And *ladies*," he added, recognizing two females in the air cops' ranks.

"Indeed we are, sir," the technical sergeant returned as he took in Lynch's disheveled appearance. "Did your vehicle break down or something, Colonel?"

"No, no," Lynch chuckled lightly as he brushed his pants off. Eyes darting from face to face, he spotted none of the SAT team members from the earlier confrontation. "My escort dropped me off at the installation's main gate, couple of miles back. I like to walk in when I'm conducting an inspection. You understand...." He took the sign-in clipboard and pen as if signing in to a new base was a daily routine. Lynch's gut instinct told him that Sergeant Tuskin had not briefed this group on the earlier contact, either. The sentry's remark about their expecting him was probably associated with some recent memorandum regarding surprise visits by physical security inspectors from either NORAD or the Space Command Center in Colorado Springs.

"All visitors are required to be escorted from checkpoint to checkpoint. Then again, I guess you're not the usual breed of visitor," the sergeant grumbled.

"No," Lynch said, not looking up. "I guess not, troop. I guess I'm not...."

The SP standing nearest the ranking sergeant played on the colonel's friendly tone. "Wish *all* the officers around here were as dedicated to the mission," he said, referring to Lynch, "Instead of more interested in brownnosing and chasing rank promotions."

Lynch's smile vanished. "Oh, it can't be that bad here," he said, eyes rising slowly after he scribbled a nearly illegible signature near the bottom of the page.

Instead of locking eyes with the airman, he gazed out at the lone runway extending into the hazy darkness on the other side of a high chain-link fence topped with razor-sharp barbed wire.

Less than one hundred yards away, the *Specter* sat inside a silver halo of floodlights. A cordon of Air Force policemen armed with M-16s stood in a semicasual circle around the craft, splinters of light extending between their combat boots and parade-rest stances. Their dark blue gun-jeep idled nearby, a constant stream of military radio chatter emanating from its open side windows.

"Can't be that bad at all," Lynch repeated in a tone that seemed to reveal a lack of sincere interest.

"Actually..." The complaining airman began a continuation of his earlier off-the-cuff remark, but a glare from his sergeant brought instant silence.

"Knock it off, Sandrowski," the young NCO said. "This is the best damn duty station west of Lompoc, and you know it."

The tight grin returned to Lynch's face. The only things west of Lompoc were several dry lake beds and, eventually, a long line of security lights that bracketed the Pacific coastline. The moon glowing overhead was nearly full, and the surf's whitecaps were plainly evident, even at this distance.

"Great choice of words," he said, handing the clipboard back. "You almost sound like officer material." The younger SPs forming a semicircle behind the sergeant erupted into laughter. "Ever think of applying to..."

"Thanks, sir, but *no* thanks. I like it here on the flight line just fine. It's where the action's going to be, you know, when the next splendid little war comes along. On the flight line. Just like Nam."

Lynch cocked an eyebrow at the young sergeant. The man couldn't be older than twenty-five or twenty-six—far too young to have served in Southeast Asia during the Indochina campaigns. "You were in-country?" he tested the youth.

"Naw...no, sir. But my brothers both were. SPs, just like us. One assigned to Saigon's Tan Son Nhut, the other at Bien Hoa Air Base to the north..."

"Ah yes." Lynch focused on the sergeant's name tag. "I spent time at both duty stations, son. Perhaps I knew them."

But he was not thinking of any town or village south of the DMZ. Lynch's mind had already flashed back to the five years he'd spent at Hoa Lo Prison's so-called "Hanoi Hilton," and the weasel-faced interrogator he and his fellow prisoners of war had come to know as The Bug. The sadist who'd removed his toenails, front teeth and self esteem, one at a time, bit by bit, in pure-blooded Vietnamese fashion. If there was one thing he'd begrudgingly granted his captors, it was their meticulous methods of torturing the "imperialist long-nosed, running dogs from the West." Tortured until they were hollow shells of their former selves.

Some of the POWs had actually benefited by the harsh treatment, developing their character, fine-tuning their stamina, honing their resolve. They'd returned to the States with a hardcover book or two festering in their brain, and rank promotions to place in their personnel packet.

Lynch, on the other hand, had not faired so well. He had steadfastly refused to cooperate with his captors, but neither was he willing to communicate with his fellow prisoners. They were always isolated, but all Air Force and Marine officers had quickly developed a system of tapping codes that kept nearly all areas of the POW camp in contact with the chain of command: back then, a Lieutenant Colonel Robinson Risner.

Lynch had been harshly dealt with immediately after his capture, and his wounds had been allowed to go untreated for the longest time. He hadn't wanted to cause any more trouble for himself than was necessary and he, therefore, quickly decided that the best course of action was none whatsoever. That included opening his lips to friend or foe. For the time being.

In cruel retribution, the North Vietnamese saw fit to house him in Room One of The Plantation's "warehouse" section, where eight or nine turncoat antiwar POWs were kept.

The American traitors living in Room One were granted good food, frequent exercise privileges, verbal association with each other, and additional favors by their guards in exchange for certain forms of cooperation with "the enemy": radio broadcasts denouncing American involvement in the war, turning fellow prisoners in to the guards whenever prohibited communications between POWs were observed or escape plots discovered.

Lynch did not take part in any of these activities, of course, but his mere presence in the warehouse's dreaded and despised Room One was reason enough for many of the other prisoners to brand the major an undesirable—possibly even a traitor—once Americans were repatriated in 1973.

He was never court-martialed, however, and even received a promotion to lieutenant colonel shortly after other POW officers began their rapid climb up the ladder toward those silver general's stars.

But fifteen years had passed since that "welcome home" promotion. That lengthy period of nonrecognition was actually the Air Force's way of slapping Lynch's wrist. The only reason he wasn't forced out of the service was because many in the Air Force hierarchy considered a career in physical security—Lynch's current specialty—as a fate worse than discharge. If they knew how much the colonel actually enjoyed inspecting the security provisions at Air Force bases across the country, they would surely have found something else for him to "specialize" in long ago.

And then there had finally been the promotion to full-bird colonel the month before. Without pomp and circumstance, innuendo or warning. No explanation whatsoever. They simply appeared on his desktop one day: papers declaring he was suddenly a single rank below one-star brigadier general. And orders placing him in charge of base security at Vandenburg—NASA's choice for the new West Coast space shuttle launch facility.

It had all come about so mysteriously. The promotion, the reassignment... the alleged cable from Xuan and the subsequent meeting with Yuri Ogorodnikova, code name "the Ogre." Yuri, who assured him Xuan was still alive. Yuri, who promised him the world. Yuri, whom Lynch would gladly kill with his bare hands if he only had it to do all over again.

But, of course—as with the fall of Saigon—the wrong decisions had been made, and it was now too late.

Before the NVA gunners shot him down over the Gulf of Tonkin, Lynch was being groomed for a promising career in his country's space program. He had already logged over a thousand hours in a Gemini capsule simulator and was being touted as the next John Glenn or Chuck Yeager, when one of Hanoi's antiaircraft crews blew his jet fighter out of the sky.

Having a Vietnamese wife was frowned upon in uppity circles of the military, but Xuan's existence was not discovered until several months into his first Tour-365. And by then it was too late to begin the reprimanding procedures: Paul T. Lynch was "down and dirty," somewhere over the North Vietnamese capital, and the rescue fleet didn't dare attempt a behind-the-lines insertion. Enemy troops were everywhere.

A squadron mate had radioed confirmation that he eyeballed Lynch's parachute shortly after the major's fighter plunged into the sea, but heavy flak prevented him or responding Jolly Green Giant extraction crews from following the silk canopy to land. Observing the type of treatment received by the downed pilot after the incensed villagers converged on their uninvited American was also impossible.

That was 1968, shortly after the Viet Cong's surprise Tet attacks on cities across South Vietnam. Even Frenchy, the Plantation's smooth-talking NVA interrogator, had been unable to get Lynch's name, rank and serial number out of him: his flight suit bore no oak-leaf clusters or name tag, only a pistol belt and the favored .357 revolver.

The camp doctor—whom the POWs had taken to calling Dr. Spock after the infamous antiwar physician leading protest marches back Stateside—splinted Lynch's broken legs and the jaw fractured by the citizens who "greeted" him when his parachute landed in the middle of Hanoi's Lake of Seven Fires. Frenchy and The Bug had entertained themselves by adding additional hairline breaks to the bones over ensuing months and years.

But still Lynch refused to talk. The Air Force officer did not want Ho Chi Minh to know he suddenly had an astronaut candidate for a prize.

When Premier Tram Pham Dong took over the Hanoi regime after Ho's death in September 1969, Lynch's treatment improved somewhat, but he still refused to talk, and his name did not appear on any POW roll until shortly thereafter, when one Seaman Douglas Hegdahl reached the Pentagon debriefing chamber.

Hegdahl was granted an early humanitarian release some four years before the other American POWs finally left the Hanoi Hilton in 1973.

Since his unfortunate and much-publicized fall overboard from the USS *Canberra* in 1966 (he was fished out of Hanoi waters by the North Vietnamese Navy), Hegdahl assumed the carefree personality of a poorly educated farm boy. Little did the Vietnamese know that, during his stay at three different prisoner of war camps over the ensuing months, he had memorized the names of over one hundred and fifty American, ARVN and Thai POWs.

Major Paul T. "Hawkjaw" Lynch's had been among them.

As he stared now at the high chain-link fence rising behind the SP guard shack, Lynch saw instead the Hanoi Hilton's eighteen-foot gray stone walls topped with glass shards and sagging coils of gleaming barbed wire.

"You okay, Colonel?"

One of the guards was speaking, the soft words intruding into his thoughts. Lynch silently cursed himself for the mental slip, and his mind filed the Hanoi Hilton where it belonged—ten thousand miles away and a previous life back in time. "What was that, son?"

"I said, would you like one of my people to accompany you down to the *Specter*, sir?"

Lynch cleared the fog from his head with a deep breath and said, "That won't be necessary, Sergeant. Thank you."

"Your DOS, sir?" the NCO glanced down at his clipboard.

"Say again?"

"Your duration of stay, sir. I'm required to note it on the log here."

"Oh, of course. I won't be long." Lynch did not appear upset that a permanent recording of his visit to the mock space shuttle was being made. "Just have to run a few verification tests on the system."

"A half hour, then, sir?"

"Less than that," Lynch responded quickly, his smile fading. "Ten minutes or so."

Was this sergeant testing him? Had they been trained to ask trick questions, look for unauthorized intruders? Perhaps they were simply waiting for him to cross into the restricted zone. Maybe they secretly hated all officers and had already booby-trapped the command post—knew Lynch was a traitor clad in U.S. Air Force blue—and were just waiting for the sanctioned probable cause to zap him. By the book. Terminated with extreme prejudice by a blue-bereted firing squad.

Lynch forced a soft chuckle under his breath and, as soon as the checkpoint gates were rolled back, started down the gently sloping access road toward the *Specter*.

No rifle or pistol discharges broke the eerie midnight silence enveloping the test site. No bullet crashed into the back of his head.

Oddly enough, a part of Paul Lynch's inner soul was disappointed.

7

Hermann "Gadgets" Schwarz stared up at the huge film screen suspended over the dark briefing room's central podium. A slide depicting the *Challenger* blasting off from its launchpad at Florida's Kennedy Space Center nearly made his eyes water.

He remembered what he'd been doing the morning of the long-awaited launch some two years ago: making coffee and preparing to jog down to the library for a little research into a new electronic counterbugging device he was working on. He'd stolen glances at the TV tube as Cape Canaveral's NASA technicians and the desk jockeys at Mission Control entered the final phase of countdown. No one had expected trouble; not Gadgets Schwarz, anyway. He had become almost complacent about the space agency's achievements, each countdown proceeding without problems, the launch always so spectacular yet expected—almost routine.

When the USS *Challenger*'s powerhouse booster rockets exploded over the Atlantic Ocean less than two minutes later, Schwarz could not believe his eyes. He could not believe what was purported to be a "live picture" playing across his television screen. He did a double take, jaw slack, but hands still moving kitchen utensils around out of habit, automatically switching off the coffeepot, tightening the lid to the sugar jar, and then sitting down in the seat facing the TV set.

Even now he could hear the voice of Mission Control: "There seems to have been a major malfunction...."

Gadgets Schwarz stared up at the slide and realized for the first time that his lower lip was trembling. He glanced around, but no one had noticed. They, too, were absorbed in Hal Brognola's unemotional presentation—perhaps also reliving that historic morning of disaster and pain in their own private ways. The Chief put up a good front, Schwarz noted. But then, he was a professional.

Schwarz was not normally an emotional man himself, but he had always been a fan of the rocket scientists at NASA. He was also one of the die-hard Trekkies who signed the mile-long petition requesting that one of the space shuttles be named after *Star Trek*'s USS *Enterprise*, and had privately celebrated for days after the unexpected appeal was so quickly granted. When *Challenger* exploded, taking her seven-person crew into oblivion with her, a part of Hermann Schwarz had died as well.

"Earth to Gadgets, come in, please."

Hal Brognola's voice probed his thoughts, calling the mechanical genius back to the reality of police headquarters.

Feeling his face flush, and grateful the coloring was hidden in darkness, Gadgets Schwarz glanced over at the head honcho from Stony Man Farm.

"Are we present and accounted for?" Brognola asked with only the slightest trace of a mock reprimand in his tone.

Schwarz nodded. "Sorry, Chief," he said. "I was thinking back to when *Challenger* exploded and..."

"Weren't we all," Rosario Blancanales sighed. Voice falling even lower, he added, "A terrible day for America, indeed, my friend."

"As I was saying—" Brognola's shoulders seemed to stretch in resignation as he made an effort to return his attention to the screen and their new mission ''—NASA has been saddled with unexpected delays recently. Even with the sudden surge in space shuttle interest following the recent lull, tests involving the new O-rings and survival gear have met with problem after problem.''

''Survival gear?'' Lyons cut in as Brognola changed the slide to the one of the explosion they'd all just relived in their memories.

''Escape features.''

''But I thought there was *no* escape the first few minutes after launch, should something go wrong,'' Gadgets blurted out, his voice immediately trailing off, like a youth who'd forgotten he was in church before calling out to a best friend.

''There isn't,'' Brognola said, quickly shifting to a NASA-enhanced slide depicting a dissected space shuttle with all of its major parts labelled and categorized. ''But it's not because the rocket makers haven't been hard at work trying to devise one. But, yeah, those first few minutes after blast-off are governed by...the flip of a coin, for lack of a better phrase.''

''And one tossed by Lady Luck, to boot,'' Blancanales muttered to an SP sitting beside him.

''I'm sure we're not here to discuss tactics involving crew rescues, though, are we?'' Lyons asked dryly. He could be as sentimental as the next guy, but involvement with any space shuttle project was obviously a mission of an international scope, which meant spies and counterspies, double agents and human chameleons coming out of the woodwork. And Ironman, still picking at splinters of lead from their last Able Team escapade, just wasn't in the mood for it today.

''Quite correct, Carl.'' Brognola's grin assumed an evil tint. ''My opening comments were made purely for introductory purposes—to give you some...*feeling* as to the problems facing NASA since the *Challenger* disaster. They've been using a lot of new equipment and techniques in an attempt to avoid any repeats of the 1986 tragedy.''

"And they've also had to hire a number of fresh faces. That's where the latest problems requiring Able Team action arise," Blancanales surmised.

"Even some of the new people have become disenchanted and demoralized by all the delays this past year alone," Brognola nodded. "They've taken to imitating the old-timers at NASA—I'm sure you've heard the talk about Cape Canaveral being jinxed.

"Well, now Rumor Control recently advised me that the President has tired of all the innuendo and space agency politics. The President wants this hex bullshit buried, and buried ASAP. But he doesn't want to push NASA too hard: another *Challenger* explosion would swing the pendulum the other way and prove to be political disaster."

"No sympathy *this* time around." Pol's harsh rasp was directed at the same airman, who nodded back.

"But the rocket scientists have assured him that a West Coast launch would alleviate all the bad vibes about hexes, jinxes and the like," Schwarz deduced.

"There it is." Brognola's smile somehow did not quite seem sincere. "And the launchpad at Vandenberg Air Force Base is nearly complete."

"The launchpad, Chief?" Schwarz perked up.

"Unbeknownst to the general public—and even to many of those in the more elite aviation circles—construction has been ongoing since shortly after the *Challenger* disaster, Gadgets."

"You mean—" Blancanales began, but the Chief silenced the Able Team commando with a raised palm.

"The countdown to launch the next space shuttle has already begun."

Gadgets Schwarz let out a low whistle that was echoed by a few others in the cavernous briefing hall.

"The USS *Enterprise* will lift off from Vandenberg's Cape Phoenix, not Canaveral.

"They don't pull no punches on irony when it comes to pickin' new names for launchpads, do they?" an Air Force policeman sitting behind Carl Lyons said as he elbowed his partner.

"Up from the ashes," the other airman replied somberly.

But Ironman was not thinking about launchpads. In his mind, mental pictures of a refurbished orbiter were forming. "I thought the *Enterprise* was in mothballs," he said. "It was never really designed to be one of the orbital fleet anyway, just a prototype vehicle for glide-and-landing tests back in the late seventies. I was told NASA briefly considered using it to replace the *Challenger* but then concluded the overhaul wouldn't be worth the cost, since extensive modifications would be required."

"Whoever you've been talking to needs to be debriefed on disseminating classified information," Brognola said, casting a wary look in Lyons's direction. "The *Enterprise* is in the batter's box. She's next up."

"Now you're talking my kind of language," Schwarz, a baseball enthusiast, said.

"If you ask me, the count's now three and two," one of the SPs whispered back to Lyons, "and *I* sure wouldn't wanna be in the batter's box, next up."

A slowly growing crescendo of murmured approval filled the room when the next slide flashed across the screen: a gigantic space station with militaristic features and the glowing initials SDI emblazoned across several solar panels took up a position over a seemingly peaceful, aquamarine earth.

"Star Wars," an Air Force sergeant whispered.

"You know the President doesn't like that name," a higher-ranking NCO shot back in mock rebuke, although the younger SP was not being disrespectful. His words were coated with awe and wonder.

"Our mission," Brognola began, "is to make sure the next space shuttle launch takes place without a hitch. The cargo this flight out will be ninety-nine percent military in nature, as, I suspect, will all future missions. And I don't need to tell *you* that the Soviets would love to get their claws on what NASA is sending up.

"Now you've all been cleared to handle Q-priority material—" an odd sense of importance filled the Chief's words "—or you wouldn't be here. I know there's no need for me to remind you that not so much as a single syllable of what you're about to be briefed on here today can leave this room," Brognola said, his eyes scanning the room during a dramatic pause. "But I can't help but be startled by all the young faces present—"

Carl Lyons's eyes were roaming the briefing room as well. Half the Air Force SPs present appeared to be in their early twenties, and half of *them* sported baby faces that appeared fresh out of high school.

These guys rate a Q-clearance? he asked himself.

"—and I *know* from experience there's a certain amount of machismo that goes with pulling security police duty in the illustrious U.S. Air Force, people," Brognola continued, raising his voice slightly. "There's a certain...*urge* to go home to *mama-san* at night and brag about the perks of the job now and then. It's hard to resist, I know. You trust your woman." His eyes shifted to the nearest female's. "Or your *man*," he added. "And you think: hell, I'd trust him or her with my soul. They'd never breathe a word of this to *anyone*...."

Brognola's laugh, bitter and unforgiving, filled the briefing room. "But let me tell you something. Nine times out of ten, they're civilians. And you simply cannot trust civilians! I don't care if it's the mother who brought you into this life, or the person you've married: you *cannot* trust civilians, *savvy*?"

Pausing a moment for effect, Brognola surveyed the faces glowing softly below the blue-tint screen. "Now who would like me to repeat that for them? I'd be glad to add an exclamation mark here and there—wherever it's needed—because I can't emphasize enough the importance of what, today, you've now become involved in, you've now become a part of."

Brognola's fingers shifted, bringing the next slide into focus: a close up of the previous space-station shot. "This," he announced, "is what the President would like to see in place in geostationary orbit over the Soviet Union's own space laser lab at Sary-Shagan within the next five years—a space platform capable of shooting down enemy missiles before they have the chance to cross into American territory. Currently it's *wishful* thinking, I'm afraid, perhaps ten years down the line.

"Space-based laser technology is not fiction, however." Brognola switched to the next slide, which was a freeze-frame depiction of two satellites speeding through space within a few hundred meters of each other. "This scenario is already orbiting over our heads," he revealed, taking little pleasure from the turning of faces that followed. "Both satellites were launched into space aboard a shuttle that orbited a few missions prior to the *Challenger*'s ill-fated flight—the USS *Discovery*, if I've got my stats right. The satellites work in tandem and are equipped with the latest developments in military and scientific hardware—developments along the lines of SDI, anyway.''

"The Strategic Defense Initiative," a grinning Gadgets Schwarz whispered under his breath. "Finally...." He'd gladly sacrifice six months worth of future pay just to review the technical manuals involved.

"Until now, neither satellite has even been tested," Brognola said.

"They've been up there and they've never been tested?" Blancanales sat up in his chair. "Why not?"

"The Soviets got wise to Project Pegasus from the start," Brognola told them all. "They warned the President that if he began testing his two SDI satellites, Moscow would respond in a 'desperately regrettable but necessary fashion.'"

"A first strike?" one of the Air Force officers spoke up.

"The Soviets would not, of course, state specifically just what they meant by their warning," Brognola replied. "And your guess is as good as mine. But I doubt a first strike was one of their options because, you see, Moscow has had their own Star Wars platform in space for over a year now."

8

"What?" Gadgets Schwarz demanded, rising from his chair. "A Russian SDI satellite in low Earth orbit for over a year, and we haven't blasted the piece of shit out of the sky?"

"That's precisely why the United States has not reacted publicly," the Stony Man chief explained. "Because the Soviets' contraption *is* a 'piece of shit,' as you put it. They've got several large lasers locked-and-loaded in a sprawling military research complex. Our people believe two of them already have the capabilities of destroying, or at least damaging, satellites currently in low Earth orbit.

"On a mountaintop outside Dushanbe, to the south, the Russians have another military compound that our undercover agents have confirmed houses a massive laser weapon. And we're not talking about something Moscow came up with in response to the President's SDI adventure. Dushanbe has been on-line since the early sixties."

"If I recall correctly, our own scientists developed a defense system capable of detecting, tracking and destroying enemy ICBMs thirty years ago," Schwarz said, scratching at the stubble on his chin.

"You recall correctly," Brognola frowned. "Basically it was on paper only, at the blueprint stage, but with some quality-control experiments that proved promising."

"Right." Gadgets smiled as his memory banks kicked in. "And the United States scrapped those plans when the antiballistic missile treaty came along in 1972."

"The United States *did*," Brognola nodded. "The Soviets did *not*. On the ground, their technology has, or is on the verge of, surpassing our own. But in space, they haven't got crap. Right at this moment, the State Department believes it would be more beneficial for us to simply observe the Soviets at work—even so far as testing. Monitor their every move, and enter the appropriate protest through diplomatic channels when warranted. And if that happens to be after it's too late, then so be it. But let them continue, for now, along the SDI testing lines. Their failures will be our lessons learned. Their achievements will contribute to our own successes. Their advances in SDI technology can only help to increase and expedite our own program. At least that's always been the plan . . . the strategy."

"Until now," Schwarz decided.

"Until now," Brognola motioned for him to take his seat. "Whether it was due to a Congressional leak—" his face grew quite grim "—or a turncoat in our own military, Moscow has found out about the cargo that will comprise the upcoming space shuttle mission aboard USS *Enterprise*."

Brognola brought up the next slide, which depicted technicians clad in anticontamination suits, working in an immaculately white, sterilized hangar. They were placing protective covers over the folded solar panels of a third satellite.

Because of the technological camouflage, it was hard to tell much about the device, but it was definitely huge. Schwarz estimated the thing would take up an entire space shuttle cargo bay on its own. The olive-drab paint scheme gave it a menacing appearance the likes of which Gadgets hadn't felt since touring a tactical nuclear weapons site in South Korea a couple of years earlier.

"Meet Peg-7," Brognola spoke cryptically. "She's the reason the Russians are nervous about our SDI program and the upcoming shuttle launch."

"Peg-7 will be aboard the next space shuttle?" Gadgets asked.

"Right," Brognola smiled. "She's the satellite that will complete a deadly trio our counterparts in Moscow are so worried about. Because, you see, Peg-7 answers only to the President."

"How so?" Blancanales was beginning to sound skeptical.

"Until now, MAD—Mutual Assured Destruction—has kept military theorists on both sides in check," Brognola explained. "There's no denying that, even with a ninety-nine percent kill ratio, a few inbound Soviet ICBMs are bound to get through even the most sophisticated SDI net. And a disproportionate number of those bad boys would most likely be aimed at the White House and the hideaways set aside for the President and his Cabinet in the event of a nuclear threat, agreed?" He paused to allow heads the opportunity to nod.

"Well, Peg-7 puts an end to the uncertainty of presidential attrition."

"Presidential *what*?" an SP lieutenant spoke up.

"Whether or not Top Dog in D.C. survives," a sergeant in the back of the room translated sarcastically.

"Peg-7 controls the two SDI platforms," Brognola revealed. "Or at least it will once it's airborne—in low Earth orbit, I should say. And Peg-7 answers only to Air Force One."

"The President's plane?" Lyons was not really asking a question, he was simply bewildered by the bizarreness of it all.

"Current contingencies call for the President to immediately board his flying fortress once there's any warning of a Soviet first strike—or even an accidental launch," Brognola said.

"Accidental, my ass," Blancanales muttered a few seats away.

"No swift transfer to an underground bunker or some mountaintop hideaway. Top Dog goes airborne most expeditiously, and while upstairs, he has immediate access to Peg-7."

"Air Force One sounds pretty sophisticated," Gadgets interrupted. "Since when has it had the ability to interface with satellites in geostationary orbit? And I'm talking transmissions, not just reception, which any airwaves pirate with a backyard dish can do."

"Air Force One will soon be refurbished with a new comp-communications bank that is currently being tested, adjusted and perfected aboard the USS *Specter*—an AWACs plane converted to perform and somewhat appear like the shuttle orbiters." Brognola folded his arms across his chest proudly. "With all that hardware at his hands, the President can oversee SDI operations as they are in the process of detecting and destroying incoming ICBMs and, as a last resort, even direct a retaliatory strike, if necessary. Peg-7 makes all that possible. She's the relay between the sophisticated electronics equipment aboard Air Force One and the orbiting antimissile platforms."

"But why not simply bypass the third satellite and have the President direct his trigger finger at the SDI platforms? Why this intermediary, Peg-7?" Gadgets spoke up almost out of character. "I'm not sure I like the idea of the fate of the world depending on a technological middleman."

"Safeguards which I can't go into here," Brognola said, casting a reprimanding glance at Gadgets.

"But Star Wars can't work." Carl Lyons cracked his knuckles loudly. "I've read all the usual propaganda against it, and feel there might be an arguable point or two there."

"Listen up," Brognola said, raising his voice. He was addressing the grim-faced group of antiterrorists in its entirety now. "I'm not here to debate the issues, and neither are any of you." His eyes returned to drill into Ironman's. "We're just government gunslingers, got that? Here to do the dirty work. That's what we get paid for. We leave all the celestial decision-making to the armchair commandos in the War Room at Puzzle Palace, okay? We're the field warriors, the grunts. We just follow orders."

Brognola's eyes scanned the oversized room, anticipating silent objections. "And if those orders seem unlawful or counterproductive, it's up to *me* to protest to the President. Not *you*.

"But—" Brognola's chest expanded importantly, like a proud cock about to enter the fray "—since I know how important it is for today's soldiers—and airmen—to feel they're fighting for a just and righteous cause and not merely some wealthy industrialist's corrupt and high-tech military contract, and since you're all blessed with those impossible-to-get Q-clearances, I'm prepared to go into a little more detail about Project Pegasus. We're heading for a world of hurt as it is, my friends. I'm not sure we'll all be around for the debriefing somewhere down the line, and I want you to enter this thing with one hundred percent motivation. Is that clear?"

"That's obviously the good news. Now get to the bad news, Boss," Blancanales called out, and a tense scattering of laughter met his words.

Grin fading, Brognola brought up the next slide. An artist's conception of several lasers leaving an SDI platform, on their way to destroy a fleet of Soviet ICBM missiles, lighted up the screen in bright hues of blue, red and green. "Over fourteen hundred Soviet ICBMs carrying a minimum of six thousand nuclear warheads are presently aimed at our beloved homeland, gentlemen. That's four times as many nukes than are needed to destroy every last one of our continental strategic targets in the event of a Moscow-initiated first strike.

"Now here's the depressing part: them babies travel downtown in excess of sixteen thousand miles per hour. All this might leave you to believe that shooting from the hip—and what the critics are calling 'Star Wars'—will not work. Too many enemy rockets, and not enough time or resources for us friendlies to take them out. Captain Kirk and Mr. Spock might not even be able to zap that many blips on the radar screen with their photon torpedoes.

"But SDI is feasible," he maintained, "and I'm going to tell you why. It's already been tested, and the test received an impressive A+."

"We've all heard about the much-publicized laser blasts a couple of years ago." Carl Lyons did not sound convinced, despite the swirl of awed whispers making the rounds throughout the dark briefing room. "Seems I recall reading an article somewhere that the whole thing was a scam."

"Maybe. Maybe not." Brognola's smile returned. "Here's where we stand now. Hear me out. Just listen to what I've got to say, then you be the judge."

"Are you telling us that there have been subsequent tests?" Schwarz asked. "Tests in deep space? *Laser* tests?"

"You be the judge." Brognola shifted slides, and the brilliant flash of a nuclear blast over the Nevada desert turned the screen a bright orange. The briefing room's walls, and its occupants seated in a semicircle before the screen, took on an eerie glow that reminded Lyons of a submarine's combat information center during full red alert.

"In 1982, the President gave the go-ahead for the secret implementation of SDI research to that point." The screen's blinding illumination mellowed considerably as the scene once again became one of deep space. "The President's pet project—currently code-named Pegasus—would involve nuclear-pumped X-ray lasers. By this, I mean that the energy from a nuclear explosion is harnessed, and concentrated into a highly destructive beam of light capable of annihilating every ICBM leaving Soviet soil.

"Shortly thereafter, when scientists at the University of California's Lawrence Livermore National Laboratory reported back that the theoretical application with a space-based power source was feasible, the President gave his famous speech that the press corps automatically dubbed the 'Star Wars' itinerary. Keep in mind that the university operates the lab under a contract with the U.S. Department of Energy.

"By the end of the year, scientists at R Division—the group delegated the task of actually producing a working SDI laser—informed the President that an experiment in the Nevada desert had provided promising.

"Dubbed *Excalibur*, some dissidents within R Division immediately downplayed the weapon as useless, claiming that, although extremely accurate, only a single laser beam was being produced per nuclear explosion. Such a weapon could conceivably win the war, if the enemy launched all his rockets into the SDI computer's field of view simultaneously. One nuclear explosion over Moscow would, in theory, destroy if not detonate all the other ascending missile payloads. But that, of course, would be an ideal scenario, and we don't come up against many of those in today's world. A one-shot Excalibur would therefore be cost prohibitive, they maintained. For each ICBM destroyed, a nuclear blast would have to take place to produce the defensive laser beam.

"The President's advisors came up with a brainstorm: use Excalibur as an anti-SDI weapon. It was well known in government circles that the Soviets were winning the race for a space-based laser weapon. If Excalibur could not be used to destroy the hundreds of missiles streaking toward the U.S., then aim it at Russian satellites believed responsible for any lasers being brandished about in space. This would still leave the ICBM threat unchecked, but it would somewhat alleviate the fear of a lopsided SDI weapon in enemy hands."

Brognola had been switching slides as he spoke, showing the antiterrorist specialists various photographs and illustrations of Earth-orbit weapons. "All the President's men—AKA: the Strategic Defense Initiative Organization—then came up with what Top Gun enjoyed calling *Super Excalibur*. It is a device capable of utilizing a single nuclear explosion to create and direct numerous laser beams of sufficient intensity to annihilate hundreds or even thousands of high-speed targets. Research immediately escalated to encompass two more national labs, at Sandia and Los Alamos, California.

"Super Excalibur, for all intents and purposes, was heavy on theory, and light on practical application, however," Brognola conceded. "The President authorized creation of the O Group, whose sole duties it would be to concentrate on making Super Excalibur a reality.

"In short order, the group announced that progress was rapidly being made along those lines. Already, experiments in the Nevada desert had produced a multibeam projection from a single blast. A lasing-rod-studded nuclear explosive, planted on the floor of an underground cannister one hundred feet tall, was detonated.

"Immediately after the blast, measuring devices, submerged in the subterranean chamber with the bomb, recorded a fascinating development: every one of the lasing rods emitted individual X-ray laser beams in the millisecond before they were vaporized by the blast. Super Excalibur had become reality. With modifications, it was renamed Project Pegasus.

"Unfortunately Livermore's Z Division—a little-known, undermanned and highly secret unit charged with analyzing data on new weapons developed by foreign countries—discovered that the Soviets were also on the verge of creating their own version of Super Excalibur. Z Division claimed the Soviet Union might even be years ahead of the United States in the development and deployment of space-based SDI weaponry. It is a commonly held theory that this is the primary reason Moscow has recently pursued a comprehensive test ban.

"We have another treaty to deal with, however, and it directly involves Project Pegasus. Thus far, I've given you some background on Pegasus and briefed you on only half of the next space shuttle's mission. The other half involves retrieval."

"Retrieval?" Schwarz brought his shoulders close to his ears. "I hope you ain't talkin' runaway nukes, Boss."

"The next worse thing." Brognola was not smiling. "The astronauts riding the next *Enterprise* flight must recover a Soviet, nuclear-powered satellite that is off course and in danger of plummeting from its orbit. If that happens, the device may reenter the earth's atmosphere, and we could be looking at another Yellowknife."

"Yellowknife, Chief?" Blancanales spoke up.

"An area of Canada's great northwest, which fell victim to a falling satellite that flung radioactive chunks all over the place."

"First we're competing with the Russians. Now we're assisting them," Lyons complained. "You're making me think the Army's Military Intelligence hot dogs are behind this caper, Chief."

"Yeah!" an airman seated behind Lyons cheered with a raised fist. The Air Force SPs seated around him were the only men in the briefing room who were laughing at Ironman's antics.

"It's politics, pure and simple," Hal Brognola finally admitted. "On one hand, we're racing to be the first nation that can boast that it's got a photon-equipped Klingon battle-cruiser in its arsenal," he said, referring sarcastically to SDI. "Yet on the other hand, Congress is ganging up on the Pentagon to cooperate with this international agreement to ban nuclear satellites that they're trying to put to paper in Geneva."

"Sounds to me like the right hand doesn't know what the left hand is stroking," Blancanales snickered in Schwarz's direction.

"There's your answer." Carl Lyons seemed suddenly satisfied. Or at least no longer bewildered. "It's the same old shit—the President vs. the politicians."

"When you hear the stats, you might change your outlook," Brognola said.

"I'm sick of stats," Ironman countered. "And I'm bored. Patience, my ass. I want some action, Chief."

"You'll undoubtedly get some," Gadgets whispered.

"The U.S. alone launched twenty-three nuclear reactors into space from 1961 to 1977," Brognola said, ignoring him. "Four of the suckers encountered trouble, and one of *those* disintegrated on launch."

"That's the one that damn near tripled the amount of plutonium-238 in our beloved atmosphere?" Schwarz's tone had turned sarcastic as well.

"One in the same," Brognola nodded. "The Soviets have launched thirty-nine orbiting nuclear reactor satellites of their own since 1965. Fifteen per cent have malfunctioned and either had to be destroyed or are considered BCOP."

"BCOP?" Blancanales smiled wryly.

"It's an old cop term," Lyons said without returning the grin. "Means 'beyond control of parent.'"

"When the Soviets announced to the world that their *Cosmos* 1900 was falling out of its orbit and was due for a splashdown on earth in part or parts unknown, the Federation of American Scientists petitioned the President to sponsor a ban on orbiting nuclear satellites. When a notable Soviet scientist joined them, the Kremlin also began publicly pushing for the treaty while, the whole time, escalating their own SDI research.

"Such a test ban would put a halt to NASA's immediate goals, which included sending some one hundred nuclear reactors into low Earth orbit as SDI's equatorial web.

"If the astronauts aboard the next space shuttle mission can retrieve *Cosmos* 1900, it will be an important political coup for the President. If not . . . well, some major city in Hometown U.S.A. could conceivably fall victim to a death rain of radiation once *Cosmos* 1900 reenters the earth's atmosphere."

"Don't those things usually come down in some desert?" Lyons asked, appearing genuinely interested for a change.

"Or the vast Siberian wasteland," Blancanales added.

"I just flew in from a meeting with the NRO," Brognola revealed. There were a few quizzical expressions on the faces of some SPs, but the three members of Able Team knew exactly what their chief was talking about: the National Reconnaissance Office—an agency so supersecret, its existence has always been denied by the U.S. government. Among other duties, the NRO was responsible for receiving and disseminating all data received by their KH-11 spy satellite. "Their latest readings seem to confirm that the *Cosmos* 1900—if it continues at its present rate—is due for reentry directly over Ontario, Canada."

"Shit." Ironman echoed the mild outburst from a dozen SPs seated around him.

9

Colonel Lynch strode through the final security checkpoint with a confident air about him, as Security Policemen on both sides saluted sharply. He enjoyed the attention, the respect, *that* much Lynch had to admit. He also knew he'd better savor it while it lasted, for sooner or later—and probably sooner—his house-of-cards charade was bound to come tumbling down around him.

The USS *Specter* sat awash with brilliant silver light in the middle of a huge, circular cul-de-sac section of concrete runway. A cordon of SPs stood around the airship in an unmoving human ring, their blue berets slanted at slightly more of an angle than those of the Air Force policemen back at the last checkpoint. These troops were seasoned pros, career airmen. Probably veterans of a counterterrorist school and a host of other survival camps. Undoubtedly second- or third-tour SPs. They stood in parade-rest, M-16 automatic rifles slung over their shoulders with the barrels down, ready to be slipped into a fighting mode at the first sign of trouble. Holstered side arms rode their hips.

On any other base, this guard-duty detail might have been assigned to lower-ranking airmen, but not Runway Seven. Runway Seven belonged to the survival camp experts.

Survival camp. The term made Lynch think of North Vietnam, and the bamboo cages he'd spent more than five years of his life inside, deteriorating both physically and mentally. One prison in particular had even become famous recently. It had been brought to the silver screen by a few brave filmmakers, only to be effectively buried at the box office by bad press from the liberal, Soviet-embracing news media. The Hanoi Hilton. A "hotel" he'd left without paying his bill or stealing a bath towel souvenir.

Hanoi. His head was playing word-association games again. The other POWs called it mindfuck. The word "Hanoi" did not call forth visions of a capital city, but brought back memories of his prison interrogators, and the few "Russians in residence" who trained them in the art of torture.

The word "Russian" flashed a file photo of the Ogre in front of Lynch. Yuri Ogorodnikova, his KGB contact. A bent-over, limping Siberian in his late fifties, with receding brown hair combed straight back. Bent-over and timid-looking, yet extremely powerful if he happened to get you in his grip.

The Ogre had first approached the colonel while he was assigned to an American Air Force base in Seoul, South Korea. He'd shown him black-and-white, grainy photos of a woman who was Xuan's double: unsmiling and shallow-cheeked, yet still quite attractive. Recent photos, Yuri claimed. Photos taken at a reeducation camp along the Viet-Chinese border.

"Unless you cooperate, Comrade Lynch," the Ogre had threatened in a calm, icy voice, "she will be executed. I will be more than happy to provide pictures of *that*, as well."

"Cooperation" had meant selling out one's country, of course.

But Lynch knew it was impossible! Xuan had perished in the wholesale, house-to-house slaughter that took place in the run-down, dilapidated housing projects known to be enclaves of American GIs during the war. She had been one of the countless women executed by the Communists shortly after the fall of Saigon in 1975 for "conspiring with the imperialist running dogs to desecrate the royal Vietnamese bloodline" by "cohabitating with round-eyed GIs." Xuan had been one of the thousands of women marched naked through the streets, bayonets against their backs, to a mass grave on the edge of Saigon, where their limbs were hacked away with machetes, their heads crushed beneath cinder blocks.

To save on bullets.

For years Lynch had refused to believe that his inability to rescue Xuan from the conquering, Soviet-backed North Vietnamese could result in such anguish. But one of her girlfriends, immigrating to the United States after five years in a Thai refugee camp, managed to eventually contact the Air Force officer to confirm suspicions about his wife's fate.

She had witnessed the executions, the woman claimed, while hiding on a nearby rooftop. Xuan was bludgeoned to death by a squad of Vietnamese who had just finished gang-raping her. The woman sounded truthful, sincere. She was adamant about Xuan's terrible fate. "Poor, poor Xuan," she claimed, tears cascading down her cheeks from sunken eye sockets. And could he please help her with a small loan? Say a thousand dollars or so?

Yuri "the Ogre" Ogorodnikova was more convincing, however. He revealed secrets about Xuan that only a close friend—or lover—would know. And there were the other things, physical in nature: the razor-thin, vertical scar beneath her left eye; the peculiar way she pronounced "American" so that it sounded like "Marry Can"; the nervous tic at the edge of one eye when she became angry or emotional; the decorative gold wire—so popular among Saigon women during the sixties and seventies—framing one upper side tooth.

Ogorodnikova was also able to recite the words Lynch personally had inscribed on the underside of each of the seven intricately carved bracelets of gold he presented Xuan on their first wedding anniversary: *I love you more today than yesterday, but less than tomorrow.* Also, a phrase popular in the sixties and seventies.

The Ogre knew her nickname for him, as well. Ace. Tagged on to Paul "Hawkjaw" Lynch not because of his combat flying skills, but in honor of the playing card most frequently drawn by the soothsayer on their weekly visits to a Cholon fortune-teller.

Few people could know all these things about Xuan unless they had spoken to her personally—at length—and recently. Unless the KGB managed to track down one of her girlfriends and, by threat or by torture, interrogated the woman until she talked. Then allowed her to flee the country among the anonymous ranks of the boat people.

It did not matter, really. So long as there was the slightest chance Xuan was still alive, he would do anything in his power to help her. Paul Lynch would not forsake his wartime love a second time.

Attempting to free his mind of the guilt twisting at his conscience, Lynch concentrated on his surroundings—on the present.

To the left of *Specter*, a shadow looming on the horizon nearly a mile away marked the space shuttle launchpads and maintenance hangars. To the right, a high, chain-link fence, topped with sagging coils of razor-sharp barbed wire. Also on Lynch's right, a narrow, winding dirt road that climbed a steep hill then disappeared into the fuzzy gloom beyond.

He was not sure what lay in that direction, but if the sign on the locked gate was any indication, he had no desire to find out. HADES—Hazardous Aggregates Disposal Experiments Site.

"Aggregates," the colonel chuckled under his breath as he shook his head from side to side. Just another fancy word for toxic waste disposal, he thought. He hoped his efforts tonight would not be a waste, as well.

"Evenin', sir." The NCO in charge of the final security ring around *Specter* snapped to attention and delivered a crisp salute.

Lynch returned the gesture. "As you were," he said. "Quiet enough for you out here tonight, young man?"

"Never too quiet at Vandenberg, sir," the sergeant responded. "The counterinsurgent and physical-security types are always up to something. Trying to make us look bad."

"I can imagine."

"I'll have to see your ID card, please," the NCO, a stocky Hispanic with a thick mustache and short black hair, said as he withdrew a small notepad from the thigh pocket of his camou pants.

"Of course." Lynch produced the laminated, blue-tint identification card.

Forearm extended and rigid, the SP kept the ID card held just slightly below nose level.

Eyes constantly flickering back and forth between Lynch's face and the unsmiling photo, the airman compared likenesses and appeared satisfied. "Thank you, sir." He handed the card back.

A second security policeman was running a hand-held metal detector over the colonel's clothing without actually touching him. Lynch waited for the inevitable beep to sound as the device neared the set of keys in his front pocket, but there was only a slight buzz and the SP didn't seem concerned enough to request that the pockets be emptied for a closer, visual inspection.

Sophisticated, Lynch thought to himself. He thought back to Vietnam, briefly, and saw himself in an old, bullet-riddled Air Force jeep, stopped at a MACV static post checkpoint.

The Army MP was courteous enough, but firm. While his partner ran a pole mirror under the vehicle's chassis, searching for hidden bombs or other booby traps, the senior military policeman insisted that Lynch open the jeep's front hood himself. "Policy, sir," he had said. "Sorry."

And Lynch had complied without protest. As he saw it, the MPs were only doing their jobs. All jeep drivers were now responsible for inspecting their own vehicles—and that included Air Force officers. It was the latest regulation to come down from the war room at MACV's Disneyland East, the strategy being, drivers would remain alert to booby traps hidden near the engine block if they had to risk death or dismemberment by opening the hoods themselves. And it had worked. Jeep bombings dropped dramatically. As did the mortality rate of Army MPs assigned to the 716th Military Police Battalion. MPs manning the roadblocks, anyway.

Opening his own jeep hood.... Lynch chuckled at the thought. *Those* had definitely been the good old days. Saigon. Pearl of the Orient. Where he and Xuan had shared a top-floor apartment in a quiet, three-story stucco building in the heart of the city. They'd watched flares float along Tan Son Nhut's edge, listened to the "cursing," wall-clinging lizards and the crackle of heat lightning as it mingled with the sound of out-going artillery.

They'd made love beneath the slowly twirling ceiling fan as rain pelted the red tile roof overhead and sirens wailed mournfully somewhere down the block. There were always sirens in the night. And there was always the threat that a random, VC rocket would crash down on them as they lay beneath the mosquito netting.

The threat but not the fear, for it was still Vietnam, and career soldiers like Lynch had long ago learned to accept the unexpected suddenness of death. When it came, it came. And if it arrived in the form of that solitary .122 mm missile, fired from deep elephant grass on the other side of the *Son Sai Gon*, then all the better—he would die in the arms of the woman he loved.

Ah, Saigon. The job satisfaction he had felt while assigned to the joint Army-Air Force Think Tank at Puzzle Palace was indescribable. Yes, those had truly been the good old days.

The collage of swirling flashbacks—disturbing yet strangely soothing as well—elicited another low laugh from the colonel as he stared at distant flares drifting over the California countryside, seeking out nonexistent intruders.

"Something wrong, sir?" The SP found the colonel's chuckles irritating and unnerving.

"No...no, son," Lynch said as he straightened his posture. "Seeing the *Specter* there, decked out in all her glorious beauty, just got me to thinking about another fine lady, far, far away...."

"Uh, I see." The SP dismissed Lynch's behavior as that exhibited by many veterans of the Vietnam conflict. "Well, have a good one, sir."

"Definitely." Lynch started toward the *Specter* after returning the security policeman's salute. "I will."

His smile faded as he left the young, innocent SPs behind at the circle of light's outer edge. Innocent. That was how he saw them. Uncompromised. Loyal. Dedicated to their duty, and proud of the opportunity to serve. Willing to die for the United States of America, if it ever came down to that.

Lynch also saw himself. Earlier that evening, standing before a mirror in his room at the Officer's BOQ. Shaving. Lathered up, but unmoving, frozen before the grim, unsmiling face of a complete stranger. He'd stared into the blank eyes, searching for an answer. But he hadn't found one.

Is this what his career—his life—had come to? Betrayal? He would go down in the annals of Air Force history as a traitor—no doubt about it—and there was nothing he could do about it now.

It was too late.

The colonel clenched his fists, trying to will away the ridiculous visions and images haunting him as he approached the streamlined P-E Orion aircraft.

He saw Xuan's face, then. Staring up at him from the black, bottomless pit of a concentration camp torture chamber, somewhere ten thousand miles away. Gaunt, haggard face lined with tears and streaked with blood, she called out to him, crying his name, hands outstretched, her fingers broken and gnarled. Her wedding ring—a thin band of soft Vietnamese gold—sparkled beneath an orange crescent moon. In his vision, at least, the Communists had let her keep it.

But he could not hear her voice. Hard as he tried, Lynch could hear nothing but the scream of jet engines as a fighter plane landed on some parallel military runway miles off, outracing sonic booms, its reverse thrusters kicking in as guilt kicked at his gut.

Lynch shook his head violently, trying to clear it of the vision of Xuan, but the sight of her black eyes staring up at him, helpless and abandoned, would not leave the Vietnam veteran.

He fought to focus on the USS *Specter* looming before him now, but he felt only Xuan's presence. And then he looked up at the streamlined Orion airship sitting before

him, bathed in brilliant silver beams, and he fought to ignore the voices screaming in his head—instructors at the
Air Force Academy, warning the recruits not to let
women—especially the exotic Orientals they'd find in the
Far East—bewitch them and affect their judgment. He
heard his North Vietnamese captors yell at him about his
"war crimes," threaten him with American-made revolv-
ers loaded with a single .38-caliber bullet.

And he could see himself spitting out at the North
Vietnamese in an open defiance that, without exception,
resulted in broken teeth or a dislocated shoulder, but always felt good. It always made him proud of who he was
and what he and his country and his President were doing.

And he could see the Air Force Academy instructor
pointing an accusing finger as well now, mocking him for
volunteering for Vietnam in the first place.

The man they called Hawkjaw stared up at the *Specter*,
eyes shifting left to right—taking in the man-high NASA
emblem on one side. And then his eyes came to rest on the
giant American flag painted just behind the cockpit windows.

Lynch swallowed hard as he approached the portable
gangway rising toward the starboard hatch. The motor-
ized stairwell seemed to beckon him, as did the ship herself.

His lower lip trembling as he hesitated, Lynch stared up
at the sealed entryway. Taking in a deep breath, Paul
"Hawkjaw" Lynch started up the cold steel steps.

He had come too far, done too much damage, dug his
own grave too deep, to change his course. Or somehow
attempt to alter the chain of events at this stage of the
game.

There was no turning back now.

10

"Who the hell *are* those elowns?"

"They look bad to me, girl—truly bad. Better police up your feminist attitude, or they just might come over here and cram it down your—"

Sergeant Pamela Pearce elbowed her partner and sometime rack mate, E. Frederick "Kip" Tuskin, but did not take her eyes off the three strangers strutting down the middle of Vandenberg Air Force Base's Commander Avenue. She and Tusk were off duty and in civilian clothes, standing in front of the south annex's beachside snack bar. "I'm not a feminist. I'm a cop, asshole."

"Uh, right." Tuskin did not have to feign the groan.

Actually the three men in question were jogging, but in an ultraslow-motion gait that was so well coordinated it easily mesmerized many bystanders. Wearing cammo shorts, olive-drab T-shirts and black tennis shoes, one was a well-built Hispanic with dark brown hair, while the others both had blond. No, she decided, one had white hair. The shade of white which, Pearce felt, belonged more on the victim of some horrible scare—not a man with such an air of confidence about him.

All three of them jogged with a military bearing that came only after several years in uniform. Or on the cutting edge of some underworld war—those the DEA or CIA were often so embroiled in.

Barely noticeable on the other side of the strangers was one of Vandenberg's resident anti-intruder specialists: Captain Nacy Lourdes. He was accompanied by Sergeant J.J. Reilly, a reserve airman whose weapons-and-tactics expertise was nonetheless respected and appreciated around the base, despite his "part-time" status.

Lourdes, a barrel-chested Filipino who'd been in the U.S. Air Force since earning American citizenship more than five years earlier, wore an ear-to-ear smile as he pointed out the base's commissary, USO and outdoor theater to the three newcomers.

Reilly's reserve NCO duty brought him to Vandenberg once a month for the mandatory "weekend warrior" meetings. He actually owned and operated a gun shop located a few blocks from Disneyland. And Army sniper assigned to an MI unit during Vietnam, he'd switched services after the war, preferring the Air Force's more easy-going reserve units than boonies-humping duty with the Army's fraternity of infantrymen.

"Officer material," Tuskin muttered under his breath, in reference to the three strangers.

"And I'm a cherry girl," Pearce replied sarcastically. "Them boys are enlisted men if ever one breathed, Tusk. *Noncommissioned* officers, minimum. Members of some elite unit. I can *smell* it on 'em, I tell ya. Yeah, military elitists. They're not the salutin' type; they work for a living."

"Maybe," Tuskin relented. "Officers usually don't look that buffed out unless they're going through the academy back in Colorado," he decided. "Lifer or no lifer."

"There it is," a nearby SP, overhearing their conversation, replied with the mandatory cynicism.

Pearce had finished her daily dose of orange sherbet, which Tuskin referred to as Agent Orange, and was wadding up the sheet of tissue that had been wrapped around the funnel-shaped waffle cone. "Well," she said, rising up onto her tiptoes before slam-dunking the crumpled ball into a nearby trash can, "I guarantee you that I'm going to find out one way or another. And before the sun drops into the Pacific in about, oh—" she glanced at her black, waterproof wristwatch "—four hours or so."

"And which one of your... *techniques* do you plan to administer, *miss*?" he asked, glancing down at her from the corner of one eye. "And may I inquire as to whether you plan on *interrogating* them one at a time, or in a group..."

Tuskin was not allowed to complete the taunt. Pearce's elbow came up again, this time striking the tech sergeant with such force that he doubled over slightly. Whirling, she then caught him in the temple with a flying foot.

It was only the edge of her foot that made a glancing blow, and Pearce pulled back at the last moment to keep from inflicting a serious injury.

Stunned, Tuskin fell flat on his face anyway—to the laughter and applause of several nearby SPs. Some of them were in uniform—sitting in a marked security police truck that a few off-duty SPs had gathered around—but no one made any attempt to come to Tuskin's aid or stop Pearce as she sauntered off in the direction of the three joggers.

"You try and talk her into some of that kinky stuff again, Tusk?" one of the airmen laughed boisterously.

After a few seconds of feeling the earth press against his eyelids, Tuskin rose up on his elbows. "Something like that," he forced a rasping chuckle.

"Round-eyed chicks don't cater to none o' them complicated Oriental techniques you got spoiled by over in Bangkok, boy!" another taunted.

"Tell me about it." Lips fluttering, Tuskin blew dust out of his mouth.

When she was about twenty feet away, Pearce glanced back over a shoulder to make sure he was okay, and treated the technical sergeant to a wink and an almost-seductive smile.

"You two sure play rough," one of the other SPs observed with mock awe.

"That's the way she likes it." Tuskin massaged a sore jaw, then began rubbing at his throbbing temple. "It's one of the reasons she joined the Air Force. 'Fly High, and Strike Low.'"

"Looks to me like she's smelled fresh meat in the free-fire zone," the jeep's driver challenged good-naturedly, his chin pointing in the direction of the five jogging men now disappearing over a distant hilltop.

"You might be right, Jones," Tuskin said, although he did not glance back at his brother Air cop. "For the first time in your life."

"Shee-it."

"Got any pictures of Pammy in the buff?" Jones asked brazenly, trying to turn Tuskin's head.

"Nope," Tuskin returned, keeping his eyes on Pearce's shapely bottom as it bounced firm and unyielding with each footfall.

"Want some?" Jones raised his voice above the second chorus of laughter that had already started.

"Anyone know who those three dudes are?" Tuskin did not appear to hear the airman as he rose to one knee, swayed slightly with a rush of sudden dizziness, then quickly recovered.

The driver spoke to his passenger, ignoring Tuskin on purpose when he asked, "Did you see the way she was looking at that blond character?"

"I certainly did, pal," the other man's voice grew somber. "And I've seen women get that goofy look in their eyes before."

Shrugging as if it was nothing to really be concerned about, the man's partner mirrored the hypothesis of all the airmen present when he told Tuskin, "I'd say they're your competition, dude."

AS THEY TROTTED farther away from the south annex's main gate, Lyons dispensed with the casual smile he'd worn while in the presence of the uniformed airmen. Eyes narrowed now, he began scanning the surrounding terrain.

They'd already conducted a fly-over of the area via an Air Force helicopter earlier that day. But Ironman liked scouting territory—which he'd ultimately be responsible for—on foot. He knew that as the soles of his feet raised puffs of dust, he didn't miss much, and he saw a lot more detail than by motor vehicle—details that could mean the difference between life and death when the black moon rose and the game became one of ultimate survival.

As they reached the crest of a low hill overlooking the barracks and business-conducting area of the annex, an entirely different expanse of scenery opened up to Able Team. On the other side of the tree-lined ridge, a maze of concrete and packed-earth runways stretched across a dry lake bed for several thousand meters. The "packed earth" was rock-hard salt.

The winding ribbon of blacktop beneath their tennis shoes continued down the hill in a snakelike, meandering fashion that zigzagged from one side of the lake bed to the other—each sharp angle ending where a hangar, warehouse or bunker complex dotted the misty panorama.

A high, chain-link fence also followed the roadway on both sides, separated from the gravel shoulder by twenty-foot-wide, cleared barrow pits covered with small round stones.

On his left, a mile or so away, a massive structure rose several hundred feet toward low, cottonlike clouds—the red, steel launching pad being prepared for NASA's space shuttle *Enterprise*. Beyond it, barely visible through the heat waves, splinters of a light blue color against the endless grayish-white: a hint they were looking west, toward the Pacific Ocean. The *Enterprise* herself—already mounted in a vertical position astride dual solid-fuel launch vehicles and a monstrous liquid-fuel rocket—reposed inside a huge warehouse hangar, hidden from view.

On Lyons's right, a flat, barren expanse of white salt and dark clay extending as far as the eye could see, ended at an unremarkable horizon, devoid of even so much as a roving SP truck. Ironman glanced at the sign hanging over a heavily chained gate: Restricted Area: HADES

"It's really great to have you guys working with us," J.J. Reilly announced as he punched his buddy, Gadgets Schwarz, lightly on the arm before they reached the hilltop and started down toward the dry lake bed below.

"I can imagine." Schwarz produced a grin of mock arrogance, but the Air Force sergeant didn't seem to notice.

"It's been ages since I last saw you," he said. "Two or three postcards from Southeast Asia or some such godforsaken place is all I've received in the last five or ten years, you weasel. Bangkok, if I remember correctly. Or maybe it was Burma. Yeah, Burma." J.J. smiled. "3-D postcards from Burma."

"Bangkok," Schwarz shot back. "The pretty, midnight-shift receptionist at the Honey Hotel on Sukhumvit Road was always chucking 'em at me like Frisbees whenever I passed out on top of a table in the lounge adjoining her check-in desk. Otherwise, you wouldn't have gotten diddly-squat, chump.''

J.J. Reilly threw his head back and let out a loud bellow as they jogged. "You always managed to crack me up, Herm! It never failed—you *always* were the wit of Charlie Company!"

"Gadgets, J.J. They call me Gadgets now."

"Uh, right." Reilly sniffed with gusto as they passed a clump of man-high sunflowers. Immediately he sneezed, and this time Captain Lourdes was the one to laugh.

"Hay fever?" he asked.

"Didn't know I had it," Reilly said, his features wrinkled with bemused concern.

Carl Lyons did not miss the latest in a continuing series of Restricted Area signs half hidden behind the green and yellow shrubs. "What the hell does 'HADES' stand for?" he asked, a concerned look in his eyes.

"Toxic waste," Captain Lourdes revealed without hesitation. "No big thing, but we don't talk about it much around here. It would freak out the environmentalists if they knew what was being stored over that string of hilltops out there," Lourdes said, waving an arm to encompass the rolling hills stretching off to the right of the road they now trotted down. "Probably half the regular public, too."

"And just what exactly *is* being stored out there?" Blancanales delved deeper.

"Rumor Control claims it's some pretty heavy-duty stuff," Reilly answered. "Requires a high-security clearance for access—one most of our lieutenants and captains don't even have." He glanced over at Lourdes. "No offense, sir."

"And none taken. I don't *want* a pass to get into that place." Lourdes grimaced at the thought of having to work at a contaminated-waste compound. "I already glow in the dark after working at NORAD for three years."

"The place used to be a wealthy farmer's ranch," Reilly added, after pausing for the mandatory round of chuckles. "Some of our brass here at Vandenberg got Congress to buy it back in '86."

"Around the time *Challenger* blew up," Lyons interjected.

"Yeah...shortly thereafter, or so. But nothing's ever been done with it, far as I know. They're just using it as a dump. Defective nukes or some such shit, probably. Chemical waste, maybe. I don't know. And I don't lose no sleep over it, neither, pal—that's for the environmentalists to worry about, you know?"

"And *they* can't get on the base," Lourdes said, producing a pleased expression.

Ironman didn't immediately respond, but he filed the acronym away for future reference: HADES. Hhmph, he thought, quite a gem, as far as purveyors of fancy military vernaculars would be concerned. Somehow he didn't think the men who came up with such titles would waste that one on a dump site, though.

"Did you notice all the security they had back there at the main gate?" Blancanales grinned at Captain Lourdes as two SP jeeps crisscrossed a portion of the dry lake bed on their left.

"Yep—" he raised an eyebrow, privately amused "—rumors trickling down the wait-a-minute vine claim the Green Berets or Navy Seals are preparing a clandestine infiltration of the base to test the quality of our own Air Force security teams. Everyone's a little tense, to say the least. It's the same old shit: war games to keep the brass happy."

Schwarz matched their smiles and, clasping his right wrist with his left hand, forced a bicep to bulge as they started down a steep incline. "Ain't no Green Berets comin' to town," he laughed.

"Ain't no Navy Seals, en route, either, amigos," Blancanales winked at Lourdes.

"Only the Good, the Bad and the Ugly." J.J. Reilly's right hand did a swirling East Indian salute as his eyes scanned the faces of Hal Brognola's Able Team.

"There it is," Captain Lourdes said with a nod. His smile had faded, however, and there was anticipation in his eyes.

The captain knew a little something about this three-man commando team from Stony Man Farm. He'd read a couple of classified memos about one of their recent missions at an Air Force base along the Gulf of Mexico, and was perceptive enough to realize they weren't called on by the White House unless the situation was fast approaching the critical stage.

Unlike the President's covert Phoenix Force, which tracked down troublemakers abroad, Able Team usually went after enemy agents within the country's borders—often participating in some of the more dangerous yet low-profile missions imaginable.

Able Team was, in essence, a force-oriented squad, called into action when some vicious criminal or military mastermind stepped beyond the bounds of tolerance and required neutralization at the hands of sanctioned enforcers partially unhindered by the niceties of legal restraint.

The Team was a small and elite circle of specialists who waged a secret war. Better-known examples of the species included the present-day Delta Force and, from earlier, Vietnam-era operations, Blue Light.

The three experienced commandos jogging alongside Lourdes formed their own kind of Delta Force. They were not formally attached in any permanent or official way to any government department or agency. Instead they were really free-lancers, working on a case-by-case basis.

Unless they accidentally stepped directly into some cross-fire fray, virtually all of their work came from the U.S. government.

Cases that made headlines—hijacked airliners and political hostages—often went to Delta Force or some equally high-profile and publicly sanctioned, recognized and accountable group.

The ones that didn't make headlines were apt to go to the men of less visible organizations.

Even in Washington, D.C., most of the politicians and policymakers were unaware of Able Team—other than cryptic references to a team that many high-ranking White House and Pentagon bureaucrats believed to be more fiction than fact.

Hailing from a secret training complex nestled in Virginia's Shenandoah Valley, below the forested peaks of the Blue Ridge Mountains, the professional soldiers of Able Team harbored no desire or inclination to imitate the duties of national law enforcement agencies, although they often found themselves assisting America's G-men on a continuing basis. Hal Brognola's boys couldn't care less about follow-up courthouse prosecution of the societal dregs that attempted to cross their paths. Alleged entrapment was not a concern of the Stony Man bunch, and prosecution was the duty of local district attorneys.

Captain Lourdes allowed his eyes to gauge the expressions of the three dangerous-looking men with whom he was jogging. He scanned their faces cautiously, as if conducting an illegal surveillance and hoping to avoid detection and capture.

A chill ran down Lourdes's spine, however, as his eyes shifted to a menacing swirl of purple and black in the distance, and though no mental whispers of warning came immediately to mind, he could not help feeling disturbed by the approaching image of doom. The skies overhead might be calm and clear, but a powerful rainstorm loomed on the eastern horizon. Lightning bolts danced about in its dark base, crackling with an intense fury that was quite impressive, as muffled thunder began to reach them.

The men of Able Team did not appear concerned with the threat of an impending downpour, however. They continued to run directly toward the storm.

Lourdes couldn't help but wonder what other dilemma they were leading him into as well.

11

"Verify the serial number, please."

Gadgets Schwarz visually checked the number on the side of his M-16 before reading it off to the pretty blond woman standing before him, clipboard in hand.

"That's what I show here," Sergeant Pamela Pearce confirmed, placing a check mark on the firearms roster, before handing Schwarz his weapons card. "Sign the back," she instructed.

After he complied, she took hold of the card. "This will be returned to you after I get it laminated." Pearce held up the small, rectangular tab. "Right now, you'll be heading out to the firing range with those men," she told him, her eyes shifting to a cluster of airmen milling about a rumbling convoy of trucks parked outside the long row of barracks. "When you get back, clean your weapon, then turn it into the armory, at which time you'll get your card back. Anytime you show up to get weapons, you'll need to present this card, understood?"

"Yes, ma'am." Schwarz fought hard to suppress the grin that kept tickling the edges of his lips. The female commando standing before him could easily be his daughter—she looked so young. But not so innocent, he decided, noting the fiery determination dancing in her eyes.

Pearce, sensing his carefree attitude, lowered her face slightly and stared up at him through thick eyelashes.

"Where'd you say you PCS'd from?" she asked. Her eyes laced with unmasked suspicion now, narrowed slightly as she inquired as to his recent permanent change of duty station.

Schwarz hesitated. The only security policemen to be briefed on Able Team's mission of infiltration were the SPs assigned to perimeter tower duty. They were the same airmen who had been present when Hal Brognola gave his slide show at the police department briefing room in Orange County, over a hundred and fifty miles away. The Stony Man chief did not want any trigger-happy teenagers blowing away "friendly" intruders should Able Team be spotted while carrying out their after-hours recon duties. Gadgets could recall how loose-lipped he himself had been in his youth, however. There was no telling how many of the young airmen—believing the brotherhood between air cops to be more sacred than bureaucratic secrecy—had informed their trusted, blue-bereted friends about the caper. It was all probably just another war game to them. If their buddies manning the antisapper gunjeeps were not apprised of the escalating developments, the "bad guys" might get through the lines, making the entire unit look bad in the eyes of Air Force brass.

"I'm just in from Texas, ma'am." Schwarz locked eyes with her upon finally responding. "San Antonio. The School."

"You're kind of old for an E-5, aren't you?" Placing the clipboard over her chest, she folded her arms across it.

"I've been busted a couple o' times." He smiled without hesitation, feigning a long-cultivated pride Pearce quickly recognized. Only the veterans of Southeast Asia managed to carry it over with them into the Air Force of the eighties.

But Pearce's own inquisitive grin faded. "Whatever," she said, as several airmen in fatigue uniforms filed past, heading for the trucks. "You might as well saddle up. What kind of pistol are you qualified on? Revolver or automatic?"

"How 'bout a Beretta 93-R, with ventilated barrel, customized suppressor and twenty-round magazine. *If* you happen to have any lying around, *Sarge*."

"This ain't *Star Trek*, mister."

"Well, then...I'm kind of old-fashioned—" Gadgets's smile vanished as well "—a .38 will do. Six-inch barrel if you've got it in stock." He knew the Air Force wouldn't be handing out Colt .45 automatics.

"They're all four-inchers," Pearce said, her chin coming up slightly.

Was it defiance that Gadgets was reading in her eyes now? "No problem. A four-incher is fine."

"That barracks right behind you will be yours." She pointed in the direction of a two-story, wooden structure that was freshly painted in dark blue, but dated back to World War Two. It reminded Schwarz of boot camp and similar buildings that had been his introduction to military life. Back then the barracks had been dubbed, rather appropriately, "Splinter Village." "You'll be assigned to my reactionary team."

"Understood," Schwarz responded without emotion.

"That's *if* you can hit the side of a barn with your '16," she added, handing him a second card to sign.

"Oh, I think I'll do all right." Schwarz's grin returned as he quickly scribbled his first initial and last name across the white paper, handed it back, then started to leave.

"By the way—" Pearce reached out and gently took hold of a rock-hard bicep "—I saw you jogging with Captain Lourdes earlier. That's kind of unusual, isn't it? You know him or something?"

"I know J.J. Reilly, the reserve sergeant." Schwarz quickly debated as to how much information he would be safe revealing. "Bought a couple of guns from him down in Orange County. He owns a rifle and pistol shop near Disneyland."

"So I've heard." Pearce nodded skeptically. "Okay. I'll see you when you get back, Sergeant Schultz."

"Schwarz," Gadgets corrected her with smile intact.

"Right," Pearce responded coldly, her jaw jutting firm and true.

"Uh, one thing I was wondering," Schwarz hesitated. When Pearce did not reply verbally, he added, "How much longer will *you* be giving *me* orders?" He tapped the five blue stripes on his upper arm while glancing down at her four. "I mean . . . nothing personal."

Pearce's smile grew—a face-saving measure, to be sure—but there was no missing the fire growing in her eyes as well. "I'm not bossing you around, Sergeant Schultz. I'm helping you . . . in-process. Sergeant Tuskin will be your team leader—that's what we call them here at the launch facility. Right now he's out at the firing range. You'll be taking your orders from *him*. Not me."

There seemed to be a satisfied gleam in Schwarz's eyes now. "That's fair," he said, before turning to walk off toward the waiting trucks.

"Oh, and Sergeant Schultz," Pearce called after him. "We're a tight-knit group around here. We get along. No politics, no rivalries, no bullshit. We're professionals, a well-oiled machine, you might say. And I'd like to see that it stays that way. So don't make any waves with the team leaders, okay?"

"What makes you think I would?" he asked with an incredulous look creasing his features.

"There's just something about you, mister. You and those other two dudes I saw you touring the base with this afternoon. A sort of take-charge look on your face, or should I say take *over*?"

"Neither, I would hope." Schwarz allowed his shoulders to droop innocently.

"Yeah, *right*." Pearce did not sound convinced. "Well, I'm going to be keeping my eye on you, buster."

"I appreciate the personal attention." Turning away, Schwarz twirled the M-16 by its sling before expertly sliding it down across his back, barrel pointing toward the ground. Buster? he grinned inwardly. Haven't heard that term since the sixties.

"YOU MISSED A SPOT."

Using moonbeams for light, Carl Lyons reached over and smeared a dab of black greasepaint across Pol Blancanales's forehead. "Thanks," the Politician muttered.

Jaw set firm, he checked the flash suppressor on his Car-15 assault rifle. "Sure wish I had my trusty M-203 combo," Pol muttered under his breath. "I'm in the mood to dance."

But Ironman didn't sound impressed. "Dancing with death is sufficient," he retorted mildly, quoting a famous saying from his favorite Dragonlady, South Vietnam's Madame Nhu, in exile in Rome these past twenty-five years or so.

"You guys ready?" J.J. Reilly asked the other two grim-faced soldiers sharing the blacked-out Huey cabin with Lyons and Blancanales as he climbed aboard the gunship. Overhead the two fifty-foot blades began twirling as the turbine roar grew.

"Ready as we're ever going to be," the smaller man— a wiry black in his late twenties, sporting close-cropped hair and a collage of scars across his left cheek—responded with little enthusiasm.

"We just ain't used to goin' out on no Lurp probes carryin' blanks in our goddamn weapons," his counterpart—a broad-shouldered redhead with two upper front teeth missing—snarled back at Reilly. The Green Beret reminded Lyons of a famous Caucasian boxer who'd starred in some feature films making the Tinsel Town rounds lately—movies about rescuing American POWs and MIAs in Indochina. The Green Beret was a Tex Cobb look-alike, except that the genuine North Hollywood heavyweight had all his teeth and a friendlier disposition. "Just ain't used to jumpin' into the void with blanks in my breech, boy!" he amended.

"And tryin' to breach security at one of our own installations kind of leaves a sour taste in my mouth," the black soldier grumbled. "Shee-it...I sure as hell wish they'd send my ebony ass back down to Honduras, where there was that certain *flavor* of impending combat in the air. Proof in the pudding we were doing something *worthwhile*! None of this pussy-footin' around and—"

"That's one of the drawbacks of serving in a so-called peacetime army," Lyons reminded them. "You get to put your skills to the test Stateside now and then—trying to outsmart the wing nuts and swabbies."

"Well, when they gonna send us to Panama or the Philippines to *really* do a job on the bad guys?" the redhead persisted, but without his earlier vigor. His shoulders stooping in resignation, he shrugged and concentrated on buckling himself in, knowing full well neither Lyons nor his partner would be able to come up with an answer.

"You ladies *up* back there?" their helicopter pilot called over a shoulder as the rotors overhead began pulling pitch. A dull thumping pop filled the air, over and over, as they slapped at the thick, sticky air.

"We're up!" Ironman called forward, but the aircraft's jet turbine was already whining too loudly for the verbal response to be heard. The pilot nodded when he saw Lyons's thumbs-up gesture.

The Huey rose three or four feet off the ground and hovered briefly. Blancanales stared out the port hatch—past the door gunner manning his swivel-mounted M-60—and saw nothing but a blanket of darkness filling the bottom half of his field of vision. Brilliant stars twinkled along the top half.

The chopper's nose dipped, and the entire ship shuddered one violent time, the intense vibration travelling up and down their bodies as if their limbs were mere extensions of the craft. Then the Huey lurched forward, ascending in a steep diagonal climb over several shadowy objects that Blancanales identified as palm trees by their overpowering, minty scent. The craft's landing skids missed striking several of the fronds by only a few feet.

A few seconds later, they were out over the tranquil-appearing Pacific Ocean—a flat, polished table of black granite. The Huey banked hard to the right, heading north.

Vandenberg Air Force Base was less than five miles away. Already, bright circles of white lights dividing various sectors of the installation were beginning to appear. They distinguished entertainment facilities and living quarters from research laboratories and administrative buildings in which the base's tens of thousands of military personnel spent their work days—and nights—bringing the United States closer to a functional and productive outpost in space.

Far below, straight rows of glowing blue strobes identified the dozens of runways crisscrossing the dry lake bed on Vandenberg's south and west approaches.

As the Huey leveled out and began following the coastline at an altitude of less than two hundred feet, Lyons could make out the skeletonlike outline of the orbiter launchpad in the gloomy distance, and the two giant warehouse hangars a half mile or so on either side of it.

In the distance, a meandering ribbon of street and perimeter lights isolated the HADES project from the remainder of Vandenberg's other official activities. From this altitude, Lyons could just barely make out a broad, red ring of lights, several thousand feet in diameter, and a mile or so beyond the perimeter. They glowed softly in the mist, probably the HADES complex itself, although he could not make out any distinct buildings anywhere on the barren stretch of land.

It appeared to be nothing more than a wide expanse of dry, flat lake bed, encircled by the red lights and, outside the ring of crimson, rolling hills.

"They must bury it," Blancanales said, following Ironman's line of sight, and thinking the same thoughts about HADES and toxic waste.

Lyons couldn't really hear his teammate above the roar of flapping rotor blades, but imitated Pol's nod as he pointed to the HADES compound. "Must be a toxic sewage pit!" he decided, lips a half inch from Blancanales's ear now. "They bury everything, then grade over it. 'Waste management,' Air Force style. In twenty or thirty years, they'll probably build single-family homes on top of it without telling anyone."

"Have some faith, Carl!" Blancanales yelled back, elbowing him gently. "The government knows what it's doing."

"Well, sometimes I wonder!" Lyons was not pleased with the words coming out of his own mouth. "I don't like the way that sucker glows out there in the middle of nowhere like that. It gives me the creeps, man!"

"Hell—" Blancanales didn't seem to hear "—we *are* the government, amigo!" He patted the barrel of Ironman's assault rifle. "About *that*, I shit you not."

A blue light attached to the cockpit's cabin panel flashed five brief times, and the pilot's metallic voice reached the ears of all five soldiers as if through sheets of windswept rain—like a distant voice calling out to them from the far side of a storm-ravaged graveyard. "Target Lima Zulu is zero-five!" he said, advising the men clad in black coveralls that the chopper was fast approaching the designated landing zone.

"Does he mean five minutes, or five *seconds*?" Blancanales asked readying his rifle, well aware the Huey's landing skids were now skimming less than a dozen feet above clumps of sagebrush at the dry lake bed's edge.

"Take a guess." Lyons shook his head irritably as the craft flared into a sideways landing across several small anthills.

Blancanales flew out of the hatch right behind Ironman. Reilly and the two Green Berets were not far behind.

Flying twigs and sheets of salt whipped at their faces as the helicopter ascended back into the sky before the five commandos had been on the ground ten seconds.

Ironman shielded his eyes with a muscular forearm, then watched the Huey's black outline rise against the uncaring stars and disappear over a faintly glowing strip of flat horizon to the north.

"This is it," Reilly muttered.

"No words." Lyons's reprimand was barely audible as he motioned Blancanales to set out in front of him. In the swirling mists, over a mile distant, dual rings of hazy light marked the northern perimeter of Vandenberg's new launchpad installation.

"I just don't like goin' up against our own blue berets," J.J. persisted. "Especially when they're armed with live bullets and we've got blanks. They're gonna treat us like enemy sappers, dude. I'm *bad*, but I ain't Superman."

"Shut up!" Lyons hissed. "Or you'll take Pol's place out on point!"

"That's part of the game!" Blancanales reminded Reilly. "We do our best to get through their security lines *without* getting caught. Remember?"

"How 'bout we agree to strictly observe the rules of silence from here on out?" The palm of Lyons's hand flew up, tagging the base of Blancanales's skull. "You guys are actin' like a bunch o' green recruits on their first bivouac!"

Biting into his lower lip to control his temper, Pol simply nodded. In his gut he knew Lyons was right. This was an odd Lurp probe, to be sure, but it was no game. And he should know better. If his time in Vietnam with Special Forces had taught him nothing else, it beat into his brain the proper way to prowl the countryside after dark.

And the weapons ratio involved was not entirely lopsided. True, they carried blanks in their rifles, but their holstered side arms were equipped with NATO hotloads—just in case they encountered *real* insurgents scouring the boonies of Vandenberg. Or happened to identify and come in contact with the American turncoat who was causing this entire mess in the first place.

As the team reached a point within three hundred meters of the first guard tower, they split into two smaller groups—Lyons and Blancanales heading southwest toward the ocean side of the compound, Reilly and his two Green Beret accomplices circling around in the opposite direction.

It was not long before they became aware of just how sophisticated the Air Force's physical-security defenses were.

"What was *that*?" Glancing over a shoulder, Pol froze in place as a distant popping hiss was quickly followed by a loud whoooosh!

The question was unnecessary, and both men knew it. They'd heard enough trip flares being set off during their time in Southeast Asia.

Reilly's group had evidently set off one of the intruder-alert devices sprinkled liberally throughout the ravines and gullys surrounding the heavily guarded launchpads.

Lyons was unsure why, but he felt like laughing aloud. Repressing the chuckle, he wondered if J.J. was the one who missed the booby trap. Was the gunsmith losing his touch now that he was back out in the sticks? Ironman could just envision the two Green Berets jumping onto the reserve airman's back over the error right now.

"At least it wasn't a Claymore," Blancanales muttered as the two Able Team vets sought cover near a sprawling field of cacti and scrub oak.

"One thing's for certain—" Lyons was no longer whispering as the first muster sirens began wailing outside the Security Police barracks some two football fields away "—now the fun's really about to start."

12

Schwarz was actually awake when the first scramble horns began blaring atop the high poles outside the barracks. He was reclining on the top rack of one of several bunk beds in the room, staring at the baby-blue ceiling. The sleeping arrangements were horribly old-fashioned—especially for the Air Force—but SP squadron strength had nearly tripled since the decision was made to construct orbiter launchpads at Vandenberg. Everyone knew they just had to make do for the time being.

He sat up, swinging his feet out over the edge of his bunk. There had been no plan to set off any perimeter alarms. Something had evidently gone wrong, he thought.

The airman in the rack below had already slipped on his boots and was clipping a web belt equipped with holstered side arm, ammo clips, handcuffs and first-aid pouch, into place. It was equipment he should not have taken off in the first place, despite the twelve-hour shifts confined to barracks.

Schwarz jumped down to the wood floor and pulled his own boots from one of the two lockers at the foot of the bed. He slipped them on, zipped them up, threw his web belt over a shoulder and headed for one of the side doors that opened out onto the unit motor pool.

Blue squad trucks and three-man gun-jeeps, loaded down with heavily armed Alert Team members, were already racing past, heading for the north and west perimeters.

"Let's hustle it up, troop!" Sergeant Tuskin ordered. His gas mask case hung from one forearm, his pistol belt from the other. With his teeth, he held on to an M-16 sling—the assault rifle swung back and forth precariously with each step he took. Though he had his fatigues on, Tuskin's boots were unbloused—he didn't quite seem to be all together.

Sergeant Pearce was right behind Tuskin. The manner in which she held on to the front waistline of her trousers made it appear that she was trying to imitate Tuskin's every move.

"Young love," Schwarz snickered as he stepped out into the warm night breeze. Already the humid air was laced with trails of silver smoke from the countless flares floating over the compound.

"Hop in!"

Schwarz was amazed to find Pearce and Tuskin in one of the gun-jeeps already. They'd jumped into a unit parked beside the rear exit and swung around to the side door, trailing a cloud of dust in their wake. Pamela Pearce was behind the wheel. She motioned to the M-60 machine gun mounted on a support bar in the back. "Well?" she demanded.

"Count me in!" Gadgets climbed into the vehicle as its rear wheels began spinning. Pearce rammed the gas pedal to the floorboards in an attempt to catch up with the other units already racing to the perimeter.

Visions of making Lyons and Pol dance between ricocheting red tracers stretched his grin from ear to ear.

THERE WAS NO SIGN of any intruders when Gadgets Schwarz and his complement of ten SP vehicles roared up to the northwest fence line, and only one or two flares drifted on the gentle wind now.

"What did you have?" Pearce asked, jumping from behind her steering wheel to confront a slack-jawed airman with curls of smoke still floating up from his rifle's muzzle.

"Out there," he said, sounding like some shell-shocked grunt in a war movie. "Gooks in the wire."

"What do you mean, 'gooks in the wire'?" Pearce questioned, assuming a skeptical stance as she lowered her own rifle barrel and shielded her eyes from a flare descending nearby.

"There weren't no 'gooks in the wire,'" scoffed Tuskin. He reached out and pushed the airman's shoulder slightly, as if trying to knock him free of the trance.

It seemed to work. The youth shook his head, squinted in the direction of the barren flatlands beyond the three perimeter fences and scanned the clusters of scrub oak and cacti. "Well there was *something* moving around out there!" he claimed. "*I* sure as hell didn't set off that first flare!"

"We believe you, bud." Schwarz wrapped an arm around the airman's shoulder playfully. "But just what exactly *did* you see?"

"Three sh-shapes—" the adrenaline rush was making him stutter "—all clad in black. L-like sappers. L-like the sappers they warned us about at the Sch-school in S-San Antonio."

At that moment, two gunships roared past overhead. When they reached the first fence line, powerful underbelly searchlights were turned on. They split up, one chopper banking to the left, the other swerving in the opposite direction.

Varying degrees of anxiety on their faces, Tuskin's team dropped into defensive positions along the boundary of the northwest perimeter as they watched the Cobras sweep the area with blinding beams of light. On both sides, additional gun-jeeps and SP trucks were pulling up to their respective sectors of responsibility and deploying anti-sapper squads sporting blue berets and the latest in heavy weaponry.

From the sandbag-reinforced entryways of heavily camouflaged underground bunkers, Schwarz and the other two sergeants on his team watched the helicopters swing around full circle. No one spoke. All eyes remained on the Cobras, which were not darting about in their usual predatory manner, but gliding smoothly in a circular pattern around the large compound.

As soon as they were directly overhead again, the belly lights flickered off and, flaring into the sharp sideways pattern, both ships froze in a stationary hover above the perimeter of glistening barbed wire. Schwarz watched with checked admiration as Pearce immediately got on one of the portable radios, flipped dials until she had a ground-to-air frequency and began conversing with one of the pilots.

A few seconds later, the Cobras resumed their inspections of the perimeter, floodlights once again blazing across the land. Several additional aircraft also arrived on-station, including twin-rotored Chinooks and a fleet of troop-carrying Hueys.

Schwarz's team was simply to maintain a secured perimeter, while other SPs scoured the terrain outside the compound in search of aggressors.

Grim-faced and tight-lipped, the security policemen around Schwarz watched for nearly an hour as their colleagues used bayonets and survival knives to poke at suspicious bushes and probe rabbit holes. One brave trooper even dropped down into a coyote's hillside lair, but it proved to be unoccupied—no hostile creatures of the two *or* four legged variety.

Finally the launch installation was declared secure.

"I saw them!" the wide-eyed sentry maintained. "I saw them, I swear I did!"

Gadgets kept one eye shut—preserving his purple vision—as a string of flares floated past, popping and sizzling on the hot, humid breeze.

It brought back memories of Nam, where they claimed Charlie controlled the night.

At Vandenberg—if Schwarz had anything to say about it—things would be different.

Able Team would take charge and maintain it.

LYONS AND BLANCANALES lay huddled back-to-back in a shallow depression beneath the hillside of thick scrub oak. A few feet away, Reilly and his two Green Beret buddies occupied similar "overnight" accommodations.

"If they don't bring in canine teams," Pol whispered, "we've got it made. But if the SPs chopper-in some attack dogs, our ass is grass, Ironman. It's gonna be *mucho* bad news for the good guys."

"Shut up," Lyons hissed. "You think I don't know that?"

Shit, Blancanales thought as several low-flying helicopters passed overhead. And I thought Gadgets was supposed to be the moody one around here.

Where was Schwarz, Pol wondered? Was he in one of those gun-jeeps, manning a hatch-60, hoping to drop a belt or two of tracer between their boots? Just for laughs, of course. Or was he in one of the approaching SP trucks, preparing to search the area on foot? Perhaps he had remained back at the compound, manning a static post on the other side of the barbed wire.

Blancanales felt his chest expand and freeze as he took a deep breath and automatically held it—two squads of combat SPs were suddenly passing by on either side of their location. They'd had no warning whatsoever—one moment, he and J.J. were bullshitting around; the next, an Air Force security policeman was almost tripping over them.

But Pol did not fear death. Perhaps the air cops would fire on full-auto at the first sign of movement in the underbrush, or perhaps they would play it by the book, soliciting passwords before demanding that the intruders "advance and be recognized." Gut instinct told the Politician that he would not be zapped first and interrogated later. This *was* still America, and not a bonafide war zone. In truth he felt more like some teenager hiding out on a school rooftop, trying to elude the hometown sheriff's deputies, rather than one of five major-league sappers, working their way into a dangerous, life-threatening corner.

But the stalkers soon passed, quickly disappearing beyond the nearest hilltop. The five intrusion specialists had not been detected. Although it wasn't as if they hadn't screwed this one up royally, Lyons thought.

An open palm raised for silence, he kept his eyes on the sky and an ear to the ground for the next several minutes. The roar of nearby SP trucks slowly faded and, eventually, all the air activity—except for an occasional flare or patrolling gunship—ceased as well.

"I think it's safe to beat it back to friendly territory," J.J. Reilly decided. Reilly was suddenly nose-to-nose with Ironman after having low-crawled up to the Able Team duo in total silence, undetected. He had obviously lost none of the jungle prowling skills gained during his Vietnam experience.

"*I* think we'd better hide out for the rest of the night," Blancanales interjected. "I don't want to go *nowhere* until sunrise."

"Don't pussy out on me, Pol," Lyons warned casually.

"Trying to outfox our own fellow countrymen on an American Air Force base is just not my style, Carl."

Pol was in no mood for additional escape-and-evasion maneuvers in the dark, and had decided he didn't enjoy recons where you couldn't confront your opponent if you encountered him on the field of battle.

"The Chief wouldn't have sent us out here unless he had a good reason," Lyons replied impatiently.

"So do we want to beat feet?" Reilly asked. "Or do we want to dig in for the rest of the night?"

"There's going to be one helluva lot of activity around here come first light," the red-haired Green Beret advised them. "The brass is going to want a detailed report from their SPs. And that's going to entail a barrack full of post-op personnel stomping around the salt flats looking for clues."

"You're right," Blancanales agreed. Pol knew when he should take his comrade's advice. "Let's boogie." He slowly, silently and cautiously slid out from beneath the scrub oak.

Moonbeams playing across his face, the Ironman snickered. "You're heading the wrong way," he said, reaching out and latching on to the Politician's shoulder.

"What?" Blancanales whirled around to stare at the sparkling strands of barbed wire sagging atop a high chain-link fence in the distance.

"You've got to be kidding," Reilly whispered, staring out at the eerie silhouette of guard towers rising from the swirling blue mists in the distance. "After what we just went through..."

"He's got to be *crazy*," the black Special Forces trooper sighed.

"We've *all* gotta be crazy," Lyons whispered with a straight face, "to be in this line of work in the first place."

"I was drafted," the black commando claimed.

"The draft ended back in '74, you maggot," his red-haired counterpart chuckled softly.

"Well, I re-upped for twenty so I could get out of going to Germany," he exaggerated.

"Save it for some bleeding heart who gives a green banana," Ironman said as he started to leave the scrub oak's deceptive cover. "Now let's get a move on. We've got a job to do, and I want it done right. The first time out."

13

"Brognola phoned me about you."

Gadgets Schwarz had not even knocked on the major's open door before the loud words reached him. Pausing just outside the doorway, he leaned cautiously around the frame until he found himself staring into the unblinking eyes of a slender woman wearing Air Force blue, collar to toes.

She was not smiling, and yet was quite attractive for a woman in her mid- to late-fifties. On Gadgets's scale of one to ten, she rated an easy seven. Long ash-blond hair was piled up against the back of her head and held in place by a long jade pin. Schwarz had purchased similar clips in Bangkok to send to family back in the States. They had cost a small fortune, and he decided that this military gal had considerable class.

Her name tag read Fletcher. The four-inch high blue letters stenciled across the glass partition separating her enclosed office from a series of identical cubicles in the building read: Criminal Investigations, OIC.

"You referring to me?" Schwarz asked, producing his most innocent expression as he stared in at the officer in charge of the base's two dozen Air Force detectives. But of course she was. Who else would the Chief possibly be calling about?

Her brow wrinkled with impatience, and she motioned him into the office without replying as she glanced back down at a pile of crime reports in the middle of her desk.

"I appreciate your taking the time to see me, ma'am." He wanted to call her "Fletch" with a smile and a wink—their private little joke on the Air Force hierarchy—but Schwarz found himself swallowing hard as his throat went dry. For some reason, he felt like a boot recruit who'd been summoned before the commanding officer because the drill sergeants found a *Playboy* magazine under his bunk mattress. Perhaps it was the disapproving look in her eyes, the gleam that warned he'd be awarded a one-way trip to Fist City if he didn't tell the truth, the whole truth and nothing but the truth.

"No sweat, Sergeant—" Major Fletcher glanced up suddenly "—or should I call you *Mr.* Schultz." There was an obvious disdain for civilians leaking through in her tone.

"It's Schwarz, ma'am," Gadgets said, running his tongue along the insides of his teeth, probing for moisture. He wished he had a glass of water right now, and glanced over at a coffeepot in the corner, but it was empty and the machine was turned off. He glanced down at his watch.

Zero-eight hundred hours. She'd probably been up since four a.m., he decided, and had already downed her quota of mess-hall brew.

"Okay," she agreed. The major had an uncanny ability to keep the edges of her mouth turned down when she finally did choose to smile. "Schwarz it is. So be it. Now what can I do for you?"

Outside, a slight shuffling of papers reached his ears, and Gadgets said, "May I shut the door?"

"No need," Fletcher replied casually. "This is a secure building. Everyone has a secret clearance or above. Besides, the air-conditioning's out. I need the circulation. I'm a Denverite—born and raised. This sea level shit is for the sea gulls. Gimme a base assignment in the 'Mile High City,' and you can have my first child, if the General ever gives me enough time off to work on it.''

Gadgets glanced at the doorway, seeking shifting shadows, but the corridor outside had fallen silent. ''If you say so,'' he relented, his grin growing. Carl would *love* this gal, he thought. She talks like a cop. ''But only people with a Q-clearance should be privy to this sort of thing, Major.''

''Shelve the James Bond intrigue, okay, Schwarz? Brognola called me, claiming you had some concerns about our perimeter SPs. Now why don't you just tell me what's eating you, and we'll take it from there.''

''Well, I can't help but remember how *I* was, back fifteen or twenty years ago....''

''When you were first starting out.'' Fletcher's smile grew a bit, only to fade again as her eyes broke from his to drift over the numerous citations and achievement medals hanging behind glassed frames of blue metal on the walls. Everything that she had achieved over the past thirty years was documented with museumlike efficiency for all to see. Schwarz noted three commendations awarded by the Vietnamese Air Force, and that altered his attitude. Fletcher was a sister. She'd been in-country.

''Right. When I was first starting out,'' he said. ''When I was a kid fresh out of basic training and AIT, it was sometimes hard for me to really appreciate the importance of matters relating to national security. I often ignored all the cautions extended my way by more experienced soldiers. Back then, the comradery and friendship of my fellow buck private GIs were more important than listening to the rhetoric from NCOs and officers. Don't get me wrong. I'd cut off my left test—I mean, I'd cut off my left hand before I'd cop out on my country, but kids will be kids sometimes, and..."

"I think I understand where you're coming from, Schwarz."

"It's just that I'm afraid there's going to be a slipup somewhere. Maybe someone guarding the towers will start bragging."

"We've already taken care of that." Major Fletcher smiled, although it seemed plastic, contrived this time around.

"How so?" Schwarz asked, his eyes no longer narrowed.

"Remember the security policemen who attended that hastily called briefing at the Westminster City Police Department down in Orange County? Well, before they were trucked over there, we had our own little briefing."

"But I was told that no other Air Force personnel would be informed of—"

"A briefing between just *me* and *them*," Fletcher said with authority. "You needed to have *someone* in a supervisory capacity on this end, you know. Someone to make sure your transition from civilian to SP went on schedule and most expeditiously—without delay or the usual military snafu.

"At Vandenberg, the whole thing is being kept at the criminal investigations level. For now. That's how Brognola wants it. The only other Air Force officers that know about your assignment are the captain in charge of perimeter security at the launchpad compounds, and his lieutenants. You probably met them at the briefing down in Orange County."

Schwarz started to say something, but Fletcher held her hand up, effectively silencing the Able Team commando. "And I don't think you'll be having any problem with the tower guards. We had a nice little talk. It was...*explained* to them that they were being chosen for a very important mission, due to their past performance in the physical-security field.''

"Meaning?'' Schwarz leaned forward in his chair.

"Meaning they've been told they're now the first team on base—an honor and, hopefully, ample motivation to counter any boredom they may encounter working the towers. They were chosen over their counterparts assigned to more glamorous duties as an indication of the trust this command has placed in their law enforcement abilities. Following the successful completion of this campaign, they've all been promised promotions, permanent town-patrol duty wherever they might find themselves stationed for the duration of their enlistment, and a thirty-day leave of absence in Hawaii—all expenses paid.''

Major Fletcher paused for special effect. And to gauge Schwarz's reaction. She was not disappointed.

"All that candy just for following the rules, keeping a tight lip and being a good little soldier?'' he laughed.

"A good little *airman*,'' the major corrected him again.

"No wonder the Armed Forces have consistently filled their recruiting quotas for the past few years. There were never *that* many perks when *I* was in, ma'am.''

" 'The times, they are a changin'.' '' Fletcher suddenly appeared impatient. "The Air Force has to change with them.'' She glanced up at a clock made of polished wood, carved in the shape of Vietnam. "Now will there be anything else? Or can we get on with the task at hand.''

"I was just about to leave,'' Gadgets said, rising and extending a hand.

Surprisingly Fletcher took it. Her grasp was gentle and feminine, telling Schwarz she felt no need to outwardly impress him or anyone else at Vandenberg.

"I trust that you and your two pals will act most expeditiously to bring this unfortunate matter to a close. We'd like to get on with the space program, you know. Launching the *Atlantis* is of top priority around here. We've no time for turncoat traitors clogging up the machinery and—"

"*Atlantis*?" Schwarz questioned, pausing in the doorway. "Don't you mean the *Enterprise*?"

"Uh, right." A strange look seemed to come over Major Fletcher. "The *Enterprise*." She rose from her chair, walked around the massive metal desk holding mementos from twenty years of duty at various Air Force bases in the Orient, and patted him on the shoulder. "Now, don't hesitate to call on me again should any other concerns arise."

Schwarz backed out of Major Fletcher's office and was instantly stunned to find Sergeant Pearce sitting on a wooden bench in the corridor outside. She appeared to be working on a crime report.

Gadgets started to say something, but his mouth refused to work.

Pearce rose, walked over to the major's door and knocked on the glass pane—the entire time keeping her eyes locked on Schwarz as an amused smirk played across her features. "Sergeant Pearce reporting as ordered," she called into the office.

"Ah, good!" The major's voice drifted out into the narrow hallway. "Come in, come in, Sergeant. I've been waiting for you. Do you have those larceny reports ready?"

"Yes, ma'am—in triplicate."

"Good, good." Fletcher appeared in the doorway, her eyes shifting to take in Schwarz's gaze briefly as she patted Pearce on the shoulder and motioned her inside. "You keep up the good work, Pam, and I'll see to it you make E-5 before the winter sets in."

"What winter, Major?" Pearce laughed, as if Schwarz was no longer there. "This is Southern California!"

Fletcher had not seemed to notice the silent altercation taking place outside her office or felt the tension in the air.

Pamela Pearce winked at Schwarz as she left him in the empty hallway. Gadgets couldn't tell if the wink meant she'd overheard their entire conversation and was on to him now, or if she simply thought he was trying to hustle one of the cuter female officers on base.

Gadgets started for the exit, wondering what direction their eventual conversation at the barracks would take. He and Pearce would surely have one later that night.

"I WANT TO SPEAK WITH HER. On the phone. I want proof she's still alive, and I want it now."

"Impossible!" Yuri Ogorodnikova pounded his fist down on the tabletop, rattling their coffee cups. He glanced around the quiet dining area of the Black Moon Saloon—located on a hard-to-find cul-de-sac on the outskirts of Lompoc, California—but they were still alone. A single waitress sat at a corner table on the other side of the cavernous dining room, polishing glasses and totally ignoring both men despite the mild verbal disturbance.

"I want to talk with her." Colonel Lynch wore his most determined grimace as he stared into the Ogre's eyes without once blinking. "Or it's all off."

"That's why you brought me down here to this roach-infested flea trap?" Ogorodnikova rose to leave. "Get back to work, *Colonel*. I'll expect to hear from you again in say, oh . . . three days."

"I'm dead serious, Yuri. This is no bluff."

"The space shuttle launch is tentatively scheduled for a short ten days from now, you know." Ogorodnikova was obviously going to ignore the Air Force officer.

"What?" Lynch stammered, leaning into the table's polished edge.

"You're surprised?" the Ogre asked, raising an eyebrow. "Well, *trust* me, my friend. You have not heard any American news media outlet announce a definite launch date, but I assure you the *Enterprise* is going into space less than two weeks from now."

"I want to speak with Xuan. Somehow. You can arrange it, Yuri, I know you can."

"Get back to Vandenberg, Colonel." Ogorodnikova ran a folded napkin across his lips and batted his thick eyelashes almost ceremoniously as he inspected his lap for crumbs from the half-eaten slice of fruitcake sitting before him. "Complete your task, then report to me personally. I am fast running out of patience—I want you to know that."

"It's already completed," Lynch stated matter-of-factly.

"What?" Ogorodnikova belched with surprise. "The data from the USS *Specter*? You have the hard copy with you—the complete computer printout to substantiate that the Pegasus programming has been altered on the tenth level?" he demanded, eyes bulging. "Then you should have brought it!"

"It's safe," Lynch assured him as he casually wiped his own mouth and slid to the edge of his seat as if preparing to leave. "In a vault at Vandenberg."

"Nonsense!" The Ogre laughed loudly and threw his hands up in the air. "You would not make such a foolish blunder, my friend—I know you too well. Xuan means too much to you, now, doesn't she?"

"It's in the form of a computer disk," Lynch said ignoring the taunt. "Five or six floppies. In a vault at the security police headquarters."

Ogorodnikova leaned back in his chair, mouth agape.

"Only one person at the SP station knows about the disks," Lynch said. "And she has orders to turn it over to the FBI if anything happens to me."

Lynch hesitated to reveal any further information—perhaps he'd talked too much already. Maybe the Soviets had another mole inside NASA. Maybe the Ogre would even authorize an assault on the security police headquarters itself, hoping to raid the vault. It was certainly not beyond the desperate Communist agent's—or KGB's—capabilities.

"Turn it over to the FBI?" Ogorodnikova chuckled nervously. "What do you think this is? One of your cheap television sitcoms?"

"I want to talk to her," the colonel repeated. "As soon as you can arrange it."

"Impossible." Ogorodnikova remained adamant. "Even if I could arrange it, my dear Colonel, I believe you're well aware that there are no phone connections between the continental United States and the Socialist Republic of Vietnam."

"Bullshit." Spittle flew from Lynch's lips. "Then have Xuan transported . . ."

"Enough!" The Ogre silenced him with a casual wave of one hand. In the same gesture, he waved to a couple of broad-shouldered gorillas who were milling about outside the front doorways of the empty lounge. He ordered them inside and up to his table.

Ogorodnikova's eyes dropped to the table's edge on Lynch's side. The colonel's hand had moved from inside his sports coat to below the table. The Ogre swallowed hard. Had he missed something?

"That's right, Yuri." Lynch grinned. "Make the wrong move, and you'll be singing soprano before the gun smoke clears. Now I suggest you call your big baboons off. There's twenty hollowpoint rounds in this baby—enough to blow the limbs off all three of you bastards!"

Ogorodnikova did not give in easily, even under duress. He seemed to be weighing his options: the satisfaction of ending Lynch's life, here and now, over the drawbacks of losing the computer disks to Air Force Intelligence and the FBI.

He seemed to be leaning toward a quick-draw contest as his eyes made contact with those of his two subordinates.

Lynch knew instantly that the Ogre was about to call his bluff. He had not come unarmed—there really was a Sig-Sauer 9 mm automatic beneath the tabletop, capable of delivering almost two dozen powerful slugs of revenge—but he was not sure he'd be able to smoke all three of the Soviets before one of the bodyguards drew down on him and dropped the hammer. And if he killed the Ogre, Lynch's chances of seeing Xuan again were less than zero.

Instead of pulling the trigger, he flipped the table over, onto Ogorodnikova's lap, just as a police car was pulling into the restaurant's parking lot.

The waitress polishing glasses at a corner table on the other side of the room let out an earsplitting scream when she heard Lynch's raised voice and when she spotted the bodyguard's 44-Magnum clearing its leather shoulder holster.

Lynch dived to the ground and rolled toward some other tables—firing at the legs scrambling about as he disappeared beneath the tabletops and low-crawled behind a bar counter in the nearby lounge.

The waitress was screaming again, and Lynch could hear radio transmissions blaring from the police car outside as a door was opened. A multitoned Alert scrambler was emanating from the cruiser's Motorola console, and Lynch could hear the police dispatcher droning on in an unemotional tone.

"Repeat . . . all units . . . Officers requesting assistance at the Black Moon Saloon on Pacific Coast Highway. Shots fired. Nothing further at this time. Repeat, Code Zero: Shots Fired. Units responding, acknowledge and identify. . . ."

Lynch couldn't resist. Ogorodnikova and one of his bodyguards were crouching down behind a stack of metal folding chairs, but the other agent—the bigger one—was rushing his position, a target of opportunity that couldn't be denied its place on his trophy mantel.

Aiming at the KGB agent's throat, Lynch fired four rounds in quick succession. He knew that, in his excitement, he'd jerk down on the weapon a bit. Three rounds did drop slightly, leaving a tight shot grouping where the stocky Russian's rib cage came together. The fourth bullet passed between his legs, missing his crotch by inches and slamming into the jukebox.

But the first three rounds did the required job, punching the Soviet back off his feet and onto a nearby tabletop, which promptly collapsed under his immense weight.

"Police!" yelled a tall man in dark blue who was now standing sideways in the open entryway, using the metal doorframe for cover as best he could. "All of you mothers! Drop your weapons! *Now!*"

He was holding a six-inch Smith & Wesson revolver with both hands—the barrel tilted slightly toward the ceiling. Lynch recognized the blue-steel pistol's protruding front sight: a Model 28 that carried six .357 Magnum hot-loads—enough for the three men remaining inside the saloon to stop a couple of bullets each.

Out of the corner of one eye, Lynch spotted the other municipal patrolman rushing bent over, along the outside windows—heading for a side exit. The colonel also knew there was a third avenue of escape on the opposite side of the building. He'd expertly reconned the place earlier before notifying the Ogre to meet him here.

Now, if he could only make it to that third door before police reinforcements arrived. Already a chorus of sirens was growing in the distance.

A flurry of shots coming from only a few yards away told him that Yuri had cut loose on the first officer on the scene. Glancing back over a shoulder as he darted through the side door, Lynch observed a bullet from Ogorodnikova's automatic cave in the policeman's forehead. The cop was dead before he dropped to the filthy tile floor. The sight of the officer collapsing lifeless across the tiles sent a wave of nausea and revulsion coursing through the colonel's belly, but there was little he could do without his dubious involvement with the shooters becoming a matter of public record once the gun smoke cleared.

Lynch listened to the patrolman's service revolver clatter across the tiles without discharging. Although what remained of the colonel's conscience urged him to go to the officer's aid, his common sense told him it was already too late—and he fought the impulses, darting out into bright sunlight instead.

As Lynch sprinted toward the Samurai Jeep parked alongside a cinder block wall behind the Black Moon Saloon, he spotted the second policeman rushing in through the back door.

"Good luck, kid," he muttered under his breath as he jumped into the Jeep and fired up its engine.

Moments later—as the colonel was spinning rear tires in an attempt to flee the area before reinforcements arrived—the second policeman was blown backward through a plate glass window by additional bursts from Ogorodnikova's Walther P-38. The thumping crunch of a lifeless corpse bouncing off a car hood reached Lynch's ears as he slowed to negotiate the parking lot's narrow entrance, but he did not look back.

Three blocks away, he managed to swerve down a side street before the first units responding to the radio call appeared in the distance.

YURI THE OGRE ran down a deserted side street after murdering the two police officers. He stopped at a phone booth as several black-and-whites raced by, emergency lights flashing and sirens screaming—but none of the officers seemed to notice the bent-over old man clutching the pay phone. They were too concerned with responding to their fallen brother's radio call for assistance.

Within five minutes, a silver Citroen skidded up to the phone booth. It was driven by a slender Russian woman with piercing green eyes and long, chestnut hair rolled up in a bun beneath her chauffeur's cap.

The woman drove Ogorodnikova to a nearby shopping center in silence, where the KGB agent went to another pay phone and dialed the Soviet consulate in Los Angeles.

Nearly a dozen rings went unanswered before a gruff voice came on the line. "Dimitri," it said, simply.

"Lynch is jacking us around," Ogorodnikova said in halting English.

"'Jacking us around'?" The rotund bureaucrat reclining in an overstuffed chair on the other end of the line wheezed and reached for a flask of Russian vodka. "I must be talking to my friend, Yuri."

"He is pulling a fast one on us, Dimitri. He just got two of my best agents killed!"

"So what do you propose?"

"We should kill the bastard, then mount a raid on the security police headquarters at Vandenberg."

"The Air Force police headquarters, Yuri?" Dimitri chuckled. "Whatever for?"

"The colonel stashed some computer software inside a vault there. I *want* it."

"Yuri, Yuri." The man on the other end of the line chuckled softly. "I think you should exercise a little bit more caution, comrade. There's no telling who might be listening in to this..."

"I'm at a public pay phone at a shopping complex. This is California, U.S.A., Dimitri—not the Soviet Union! Listen to me," Ogorodnikova snapped. "The best time to assault the SP headquarters would be between zero-three hundred and zero-four hundred, when there's no one present but the duty officer, a desk sergeant, two turnkeys and the base prisoners. At that time of night, they'll have everyone else out rattling doorknobs at the BX and commissary."

"I'll take your suggestion under advisement, comrade."

Disappointment mingled with anxiety in Ogorodnikova's sagging eyes. He was not expecting this sort of delay. "When will I hear from you again?" he asked. "I was hoping to mount the sapper attack tonight—tomorrow at the latest. There are only nine days remaining until the *Enterprise* is launched, you know."

"We will be in touch, Yuri."

A click and then a dial tone filled Yuri the Ogre's ear.

"THIS IS REALLY TURNING into a creepy job," J.J. Reilly complained. "First they hold me over on reserve status— not that I don't enjoy your dudes' company, to be sure— but then we get this cryptic message from *your* boss—" he motioned in Lyons's direction "—and now you tell me

Vandenberg should expect an actual sapper attack sometime soon. Hell, gentlemen, this is Southern California—
not South Vietnam.''

The men were sitting on concrete slabs behind the armory, cleaning their weapons, and Gadgets Schwarz
slapped an empty banana clip into his Car-15 before saying, ''Look, J.J., there are only eight days left until the
Enterprise is launched. Eight days in which we've gotta
keep on our toes and, if the situation calls for it, mix it up
with Ivan The Hun again—now that's not so bad, is it?
You're the gunsmith. You *like* gunplay, don't you?''

''Thanks for nothing,'' Reilly scoffed. He turned to
Captain Lourdes, who was browsing through an Air Force
technical manual on gyroscopes. ''What about you,
Cap'? Is this a ration of shit, or *what*?''

''Look, J.J.,'' Lourdes started without looking up from
the blueprints in his book, ''like Schwarz said, there are
eight lousy days to go. Hell, you're a virtual short-timer,
my man. Consider it summer camp.''

''Tell that to my reserve unit commander.''

''I will,'' Lourdes said with a smile. ''If you feel it's
necessary. Hey, look at me—I've got patience. Two college degrees in astronomy and space medicine, and what
does the Air Force have me doing? Physical-security
specialist at a dry salt lake bed.''

''Maybe so, but you're also on the waiting list.'' Reilly
didn't sound like he was fooled.

''Waiting list?'' Blancanales asked, glancing up from
his unassembled assault rifle.

When Lourdes shrugged modestly, J.J. explained for
him. ''The Captain's on the waiting list for astronaut
training.''

''Actually, I've already taken a number of strenuous
training course that will eventually lead to astronaut status,'' Lourdes revealed. ''In my spare time.''

"About four thousand *hours* of that free time," Reilly boasted proudly.

"Maybe you'll get lucky," Ironman said matter-of-factly, "and get to fly the first orbiter shot into space since the *Challenger* explosion."

"With only eight days to go until the *Enterprise* launch?" Reilly laughed. "Hardly!"

"You never know." Lourdes grinned as if he was holding back on the men. Could a security police captain who'd been working back-to-back shifts on the dusty perimeter for the past six months be preparing for an important NASA mission?

"I just wish we could find out who the traitor is—who it is who's cooperating with the Commies to destroy the shuttle program before it even gets back off the ground," J.J. commented, shifting gears on them again.

"Don't forget SDI," Blancanales reminded Reilly. "If the *Enterprise* fizzles, Star Wars comes crashing down on us as well."

"You've certainly got a way with words, Pol."

"Until the trenchcoat types in Criminal Investigations and Air Force Intelligence discover who's feeding information to the Soviets," Lourdes began slamming his book shut, "there's not much we can do about it."

"Except keep our eyes open," Gadgets said. "And continue to test the Alert Teams with night probes. Speaking of prowlers—" he locked an accusing set of eyes on Lyons "—where are your two Green Beret buddies?"

"Traitors, spies, KGB?" A female voice turned every head in her direction. Sergeant Pearce stepped out from between a stack of storage boxes and said, "And who the hell are *these* characters?" Her eyes scanned Blancanales and Lyons while her words lashed out at Schwarz.

"Friends," he responded quickly. "Assigned to another SAT team. On the other side of base."

"*Now* I remember." Her eyes shifted to Lourdes. "Good afternoon, sir." Pearce was in uniform, her blue beret cocked smartly to the right, and she brought her hand up in a crisp salute.

Blancanales swallowed hard. Had she seen their faces the night before—when he and Lyons and the two Green Berets were prowling the perimeter?

"You're the two playboys who were out joggin' with Schultz here and the Captain a few days ago," Pearce answered his thought with amused words that brought unbelievable relief. "Out on the south perimeter, right?"

"It's Schwarz," Gadgets corrected her. "*Sergeant* Schwarz, if you don't mind. A little discipline around here wouldn't hurt this unit, you know."

Pearce didn't seem to be listening. "Now why don't you guys be real sweethearts and let me in on the big secret: traitors, spies, KGB? Come on! My lips are sealed." The gleam of restrained humor left her eyes. "Pam Pearce can keep a secret."

"Looks like we don't have much of a choice," Lyons said.

"Of course we do." Lourdes stood up, and the woman backed off a few paces. "I can have her insubordinate ass locked up in solitary confinement until this whole thing is over with." The small wiry Filipino-born officer suddenly seemed seven feet tall.

"You'd treat her like that after the way she risked her life out on the perimeter last night?" Schwarz asked, lifting his chin slightly in disbelief. "Come on, Cap'."

"Well...."

Lourdes knew the Able Team commando had a point. Much as he hated to, the Air Force captain gave in to Gadgets's subtle persuasion.

So they told her about the turncoat and the scuttlebutt that he—or she—was trying to do everything possible to prevent the *Enterprise* launch next week and, failing that, bring it down in a ball of flames.

"I'VE BEEN THINKING about something," Pearce said, approaching Lyons and the others at the BX coffee shop later that evening. She had changed into a curve-revealing blouse and skirt. "It's really been bothering me and I'd like to get it off my chest."

"Shoot," Gadgets said, pouring an inky cup of brew that he let overfill his cup as he admired her figure. He hastily wiped off the steaming liquid, then handed her the cup.

Lyons and Blancanales smiled with approval when she downed the entire cup without the aid of cream or sugar.

"I've been thinking about what you told me earlier—about the traitor in our midst. And something came to mind...."

"We're all ears, Sarge," Ironman said, leaning back in his folding metal chair, head resting in clasped hands.

"It happened just before you guys showed up. Out on the perimeter. Inside the fence line, actually—near Runway Seven. We were responding to a tower rat report of a possible intruder in Sector Fourteen. Me, Tusk and our Alert Team. We intercepted an officer moving through the boonies on foot."

"An Air Force officer?" Blancanales sat up in his seat.

"Right. The guy was acting real strange. Out of place, you know?"

"Was he wearing cammies?" Schwarz asked.

"No," Pearce shook her head. "Air Force blue, all the way. Class As, in fact—without the jacket. And he was armed. Carried a Colt .45."

"Your people filed a report on the incident?" Lyons asked.

"Of course," she nodded. "Well, at least Tuskin was supposed to." She seemed to reconsider. "Yes, I'm sure he did. But I doubt if anybody ever really read it."

"And why is that?"

"Because we were expecting intruders. *Mock* sappers. You know: Navy Seals, out to breech our perimeter and make the SPs look bad. Green Berets trying to penetrate the new launchpad facilities—steal a NASA flag or something. Even an Air Force colonel sent by the Space Command in Colorado Springs to inspect our security arrangements."

"And what was the colonel's name?" Lyons asked solemnly.

"I don't remember, exactly. Tusk would know. But everyone else seemed to know him. They called him...Hawkjaw."

Ironman turned to advise Schwarz, "Get over to Major Fletcher's office, Gadgets. Have her run the alias *Hawkjaw* through her OSI computers. I want everything that comes back on whoever belongs to that nickname: his personnel file, an ID photo...even a fingerprint card would help—*especially* a fingerprint card."

"You got it!"

THE BIG MAN chomped on the Honduran cigar before returning his concentration to the data just in from Aaron Kurtzman.

Stony Man's chief of operations and liaison with Washington bureaucracy was older than most of the men who worked under him, and supervisory responsibilities had tacked perhaps a few more years to his appearance, but Brognola was still as energetic as ever. He studied the radio logs and data scans, glancing back at the file photo of Colonel Lynch, before reviewing the enclosed reports.

Now and then he scribbled notes in his own indecipherable shorthand. Finally he went over the activity summary from NASA for a third time.

The phone rang as he was reaching for a fresher cigar, and Brognola did not hesitate to answer it. He immediately recognized the voice on the other end.

"Yes, Mr. President." His eyes narrowed as he digested the suggestions being fielded by one of the shuttle's biggest fans—the man in the White House. "Yes, sir. It's a risky plan, sir, but it might work. This KGB thing is beginning to worry me, too. I'll get right on it, sir."

He hung up the phone and proceeded across the cavernous ground-floor room to a phone hookup attached to the opposite wall. Brognola began pacing the nerve center of Stony Man Farm as he waited for his long-distance call to be put through to the West Coast.

The scrambled connection to Vandenberg Air Force Base finally went through. "Carl, Brognola here. Give me a situation report, and don't leave anything out."

Leaning against a giant map of Indochina but concentrating on a series of scars running across the knuckles of his gun hand, Brognola listened intently for over a minute before responding to Ironman's briefing.

"You say his name's Lynch? Okay. That confirms it. I just spoke with the President. I'll keep you posted."

Without waiting for a comment from Lyons, Brognola broke the connection and began dialing another series of coded access numbers. "Bear? Brognola here. Get me everything you can on one Air Force Colonel Lynch, Paul T. What? No, just hold on to it. I'll be there in less time than it took for Saigon to fall!"

He slammed down the phone, poked his head into a dimly lighted corridor, and yelled out, "Grimaldi!"

"Yeah, boss?" A stocky man with wavy black hair came running from the other end of the hallway.

"Get my plane ready, ASAP! We're heading back to Vandenberg."

14

Colonel Lynch was nowhere to be found. Able Team had searched the entire base for the Air Force officer, but he seemed to have vanished as mysteriously as he had first appeared.

"We really never had anything on him," Schwarz conceded.

"But I sure would like to have had a talk with the man," Lyons muttered. "Brognola's en route to brief us on something—I just spoke with him on the plane patch. But then he's off to Colorado Springs. He's going to run a little background check on Hawkjaw, to make sure he's who he claims he is . . . or was."

"Maybe he is . . . *was* a security inspector, like he said," Blancanales offered.

"Who's side are you on?" Gadgets asked elbowing the Politician lightly.

The three Able Team commandos stared out at the *Enterprise* as it stood in a vertical position atop dual solid-fuel boosters and a monstrous liquid-propellant tank. NASA technicians had recently rolled the orbiter out of its massive construction hangar toward the recently completed launchpad. Tonight a full moon hung over the mist-enshrouded horizon, behind and slightly above the *Enterprise*.

"She sure is a beauty," Gadgets said.

Schwarz and his two counterparts were standing on the southern perimeter of Vandenberg's missile test site, nearly a mile away, but the orbiter and her launchpad were so huge that their outlines against the moonlit night were clearly visible.

"We've got trouble!" Lyons shouted as intruder sirens began screaming several hundred yards down the road—near a guard tower that suddenly went black. "Let's move it!"

They hopped into the gun-jeep parked a few feet away and roared off down the steep incline, away from the launch facilities, just as a blinding explosion erupted beneath the guard tower.

"We've got movement in the—" a voice started to advise over the radio band, but the transmission abruptly ended, and static rushed in to reclaim the net.

Schwarz grabbed the microphone hanging from their jeep's dash and called in the situation as Lyons guided the vehicle toward the fireballs and smoke rising in the distance. "This is Alpha One!" he said, squeezing the transmit lever until the handset cracked slightly under the pressure. "We're approaching Post Six Alpha Charlie, do you copy? Six Alpha Charlie appears to be under some sort of attack. We observe explosions at that location and are en route!"

"Roger, Alpha One. Dispatching an Alert Reactionary Force at this time. They'll be coming in from the south, over."

"Shit," Blancanales whispered under his breath as a blast of white phosphorous erupted where the guard tower had once been standing. The brilliant bits of glowing particles climbed the skyline, mushroomlike, then showered down on the land, igniting a brush fire.

ALL THREE SPs WERE DEAD, burned in the explosion. There was no sign of any intruder, but if Air Force investigators initially tried to play the incident down as an accidental explosion, that theory was quickly discarded when it was noted that the security policemen did not carry Claymores or willie peter. And that their weapons were missing.

Able Team, along with dog handlers and a search squadron, scoured the perimeter fence line on both sides for several miles, but failed to find so much as a single boot print.

It was, of course, possible that the violent probe was related to the upcoming launch of the *Enterprise*. There was no other obvious purpose or goal behind the assault. "Unless the Commies were testing our response time," Gadgets ventured a hypothesis.

Lyons wondered if the murders were connected with the disappearance of Hawkjaw.

SIX MORE SPs turned up dead the following night. Their guard towers were blown off the face of the earth—only charred splinters and a few molten gun turrets remained. As with the previous night assaults, their weapons had been taken, and the sappers had left no tracks in the dry salt lake bed. Mock probes by Able Team were cancelled. Major Fletcher's tower guards were given express permission to shoot any shadows on sight.

"I don't think this Hawkjaw character is behind the bombings," Schwarz told Lyons and Blancanales afterward, while they were cruising the perimeter aboard a gun-jeep, eyes scanning the barren wastes beyond the barbed wire. "In fact, I think he might have fallen victim to whoever's killing our Air Force SPs."

"Don't worry about the colonel," Lyons told him. "Worry about the press finding out about the bombings. I can't believe the news blackout has been effective."

"We're out in the middle of nowhere," Blancanales reminded Ironman. "In the heart of a missile-testing range. That helps."

"I guess it does," Lyons said, glancing over at a reflectorized "keep out" sign hanging from a section of secondary fence line that separated the launch facilities from a barren stretch of flatlands that extended off to the east.

"Let's get out of here," Lyons ordered.

A loud *whooosh!* in the distance silenced the Ironman.

"Flare," Schwarz whispered. "Let's go!"

The flare burst some five hundred yards down line from where they were parked, on the other side of the perimeter. It was about fifty yards out from the barbed wire.

Lyons brought the gun-jeep up in a sideways skid beside the guard tower involved, as SPs manning the raised static post sent steady streams of M-60 machine-gun fire down into moving shadows that darted about between shrubs and cacti sprouting in the dry lake bed.

Rolling from their jeep, Lyons and Schwarz dropped into prone positions under the lowest strands of barbed wire and began firing short, three- and four-round bursts at the disoriented intruders.

Back in the jeep, Blancanales remained behind the M-60. Like the SPs above, he was sending solid beams of red tracer out to scour the landscape. More than a few zigzagging shapes were blown off their feet and thrust through the air.

Five gunships responded to the area within minutes, first disintegrating the sector with minigun and rocket fire, then bathing nearly every square foot of lake bed with blinding floodlights.

The silver beams revealed a six-man Soviet R-team—or what was left of it—lying about the blood-soaked salt flats.

There would be no prisoners to interrogate.

COLONEL LYNCH DEBATED picking up the ringing phone. No one knew about the apartment that was secreted within a dilapidated housing project on the east side of Lompoc. He'd had the phone installed for calling out only. Who would be calling in?

"Five-four-six-eight," he said, giving the last four digits of his phone number, after his curiosity got the best of him.

"Colonel, how are you?"

"Yuri?" Lynch's mind flashed back to the confrontation and shoot-out at the Black Moon Saloon. "How did you get this number?"

Ogorodnikova laughed loudly into his mouthpiece. "No hard feelings, my dear Colonel Lynch? After all, a little gunplay each day keeps the old age away, no?"

"I asked you how you got this number!"

"It is not important." Yuri's voice grew stern. "Now listen. I will not be calling back to make this offer twice."

"I'm listening," Lynch gritted his teeth, expecting a setup. But he really had no choice—Yuri's KGB agents could be outside right now, watching him, preparing to pounce.

"Dimitri has had a change of heart."

"Dimitri?" Lynch knew this was not the time to be asking questions.

"We have decided to allow you to correspond with your wife."

"Xuan?" Lynch thought his heart would stop on him then and there. "Xuan is truly alive?"

"Of course she is." Ogorodnikova's chuckle came across the phone lines like a death-bed rattle. "We have a letter from her for you. A letter and a photograph."

"And what will this cost me, Yuri?" Lynch fought to control his excitement.

"The evidence. The computer disks you have placed inside the security vault at SP headquarters. The duplicate of the Skylink microwave directives. Deliver the disks, and we will provide you with an address where your wife can be reached."

"The letter and photograph first."

"Of course." Yuri's chuckle took on a sinister tone. "Proceed to the contract post office at Main and Fifth Streets in Lompoc. Taped beneath the only table in the lobby will be a key. It will fit postal box number 31754. Inside the box will be a plain brown envelope. I expect to be hearing from you within twenty-four hours, comrade."

That depends on what Xuan has to say, Lynch thought as he hung up the phone. He lifted the Colt .45 from a nearby nightstand, slipped it into his shoulder holster and left the apartment.

HAL BROGNOLA TURNED from the chalkboard in response to Lyons's persistent questions about Hawkjaw Lynch. "Forget about the colonel," he said. "Lynch has not reported back to his duty station in Colorado Springs. No one's sure where the hell he is. At least no one's talking to *me*. But the Air Force refuses to carry him as AWOL, and the colonel's a big boy. He'll be okay. Besides, he's small fish in the overall scheme of things," Brognola said pointing to the chalkboard words that Gadgets Schwarz, head tilted to one side, was trying to make out, "and we have more important things to concern ourselves with right now, gentlemen. For instance, something big may possibly go down aboard the shuttle itself. Exactly *what*, we don't know, but..."

"Aboard the *Enterprise*, Chief?" Blancanales sat ramrod straight in his chair between the other members of Able Team—the only other men attending Brognola's hastily called briefing at the Vandenberg Air Police Squadron Headquarters.

"Right. And guess who's going to prevent all hell from breaking loose in outer space?" Brognola beamed as he rocked back slightly on his heels.

"You're shittin' us." Lyons, who had been standing up, sat down heavily.

"I wouldn't shit you, Ironman—you're my favorite turd."

"But Chief—" Gadgets started to protest.

"You guys just became astronauts," Brognola announced without fanfare.

"This ain't funny," Blancanales said somberly.

"And I ain't no comedian," Brognola replied. "The three of you will be aboard the *Enterprise* when it lifts off in five days from Vandenberg's Cape Phoenix."

"I don't even know how to fly Grimaldi's collection of paper airplanes," Lyons said. "How can you expect us to—"

"You'll be passengers," Brognola explained. "The orbiter is basically a computer-operated spacecraft. Pilots aren't even needed for the launch—they're simply seat warmers. Nor are they really required for the return glide to earth, although NASA humors the astronauts so they'll feel useful, I suppose. Your job will be to provide security aboard the *Enterprise*. The other three occupants will be bonafide astronauts—charged with manning the cockpit controls, and all payload experiments. And that includes recovery of the *Cosmos* 1900 nuclear satellite—if the mission proceeds that far."

"What do you mean *if*?" Blancanales cut in.

"Did you say *five* days, Chief?" Lyons asked.

"You heard right." Brognola pulled a large set of blueprints and satellite photos from his briefcase and tacked them to the bulletin board. "Gentlemen," he began, "this is the Russian version of our space shuttle. It's known as *Kosmolet*, or Space Flyer. Ten of the hummers are currently housed inside giant hangars at the Baikonur Cosmodrome near Leninsk."

"One has recently been moved out toward a launch-pad."

"The design sure looks familiar," Lyons said, shifting his eyes toward Schwarz. "Do you think there might be just a bit of cheating going on here? A mole in our midst, perhaps?"

Brognola ignored the veiled reference to Colonel Lynch. "We already thought about that," he said. "Like our orbiter, the Soviets' *Kosmolet* is white on top with black heat tiles on bottom. It has the exact same delta-wing shape and raked tail. Our satellite recon photos show it to be a hundred and twenty-five feet long, and boasting a seventy-six-foot wingspan."

"That's identical to our shuttle," Gadgets said.

"Just about," Brognola corrected him. "There are only a couple of other significant differences between the U.S. and Soviet orbiters. The *Kosmolet*'s wingtips appear more squared, and the tail section does not support the trio of engines that assist the shuttle during launch.

"*Glavkosmos* has announced that an atmospheric launch window will open next week and close shortly thereafter. They are going to launch their *Kosmolet* on Monday."

"That's six days from now," Blancanales quickly calculated.

"That's why we go in five," Gadgets surmised. "To make the U.S. space shuttle program look good—to beat the Russians back into orbit."

"Well, they've still got their *Mir* and *Salyut 7* space stations in place, of course," Brognola said. "But, basically, you're right on target."

"This is incredible," Blancanales said. "It's unbelievable."

"Believe it," Brognola shot back. "And get used to the idea. As of seventeen hundred hours today, you three guys are apprentice astronauts. I'll have official orders cut for you within the hour. Report for a crash training course at the NASA flight lab, located in Sector Four, *now*. You've got T minus a little over a hundred or so hours until launch, ladies," Brognola smiled. "Be sure and send me back a postcard...."

"Finally," Gadgets mused. "My day in the media spotlight."

"Not quite." The Chief's smile vanished. "This launch is ninety-nine percent military in payload. No spectators. No press. It's closed to the public, period."

"I guess I've got the right stuff after all," Blancanales mumbled as he followed Lyons and Schwarz back to the barracks.

"ANYBODY SEEN CAPTAIN LOURDES around lately?" Schwarz asked Blancanales as they headed toward the NASA flight lab for their third day of weightlessness training.

"Pearce mentioned that he got a sudden transfer—hastily arranged," Lyons revealed as they reached their classroom.

Inside the small room, General Farthing was waiting. He greeted the three veteran commandos with a warm smile and handshake, then immediately commenced updating them on the progress—or deterioration—of the Soviet nuclear-powered satellite.

"The *Cosmos* 1900 weighs nearly four and one half tons," Farthing said. "It was launched back in December of '87, but the Russians lost radio contact with it less than five months later, which prevented ground-ordered boost of the satellite to a higher, more stable orbit.

"I can't emphasize enough how important this shuttle mission is. A little over ten years ago, another Soviet nuclear-powered satellite crashed down into the tundra of northern Canada, contaminating some forty thousand square miles of land.

"The *Enterprise* must be able to recover the *Cosmos* before its orbit erodes. Not only is there danger from contamination—especially if the satellite should come down in the heart of a major American city—but there's a terrorist threat as well."

"A terrorist threat?" Pol's eyes lighted up. "Now you're talkin' our area of expertise, General."

"If the satellite's fuel core lands in large pieces, over a hundred and ten pounds of enriched uranium 235 could become available for professional scavengers—until authorities arrived on the scene, of course."

"But is this thing really such a threat?" Lyons asked. "Won't it just burn up in the atmosphere if we don't get to it in time?"

"*Cosmos* 1900 will not break up on reentry," Farthing said, sounding convinced. "The satellite has a hard-shelled, cylindrical housing that will act as a heat shield of sorts for the reactor core during the plunge to earth. Chunks as big as those from *Skylab* are unlikely—but there *will* be debris.

"And this is not that uncommon." Farthing leaned onto his podium as he locked eyes with Ironman. "The Russians have had six major failures out of the last thirty-three nuke satellites—mostly with their Rorsat series, or radar ocean recon satellites, which they use to monitor our navy. I can't emphasize enough how important this upcoming shuttle launch is going to be."

"This satellite we're taking up," Gadgets said. "This Project Pegasus deal. I'm getting the impression it's an SP-100 model, also nuclear powered."

Farthing shook his head vigorously. "No, no, no," he said. "Don't confuse Pegasus with the SP-100, which is still in development for NASA, SDI and the Department of Energy. The SP-100 is a hundred-kilowatt nuclear-powered reactor costing seven hundred million dollars, which will eventually be the powerhouse for SDI. It's not due to go up until the mid-1990s.

"If the SP-100 is ever launched, it will be only the second nuclear reactor put into space by the U.S. Nearly twenty-five years ago, NASA launched an experimental *Snapshot* satellite into Earth orbit, but it malfunctioned in less than two months and remains in space, circling eight hundred miles above the Earth."

"But we were told—" Schwarz began.

Farthing waved him silent. "You're think about a RTG. Radioisotope thermoelectric generators, of which the U.S. has launched twenty two, and the Soviets eight or nine—that we know about. The uranium in the reactors is harmless until quite a while after the launch phase of the mission is completed. But the RTG's plutonium is highly toxic from the instant it's loaded into a payload configuration. Any more questions?" Farthing's eyes scanned the blank faces sitting before him. "Good. Then, let's move on to the subject of using the latrine in zero gravity."

"I get the feeling we're gonna glow in the dark after this whole thing is over," Blancanales whispered.

Lyons stared straight ahead when he said, "*If* we make it back."

LYNCH STARED DOWN at the grainy, black-and-white photograph that had been waiting for him in the post office drop box. He reread the one-page letter for the tenth time, convinced now that it had not been written by Xuan.

It was a forgery.

The photo had to be more than ten years old, and probably dated back to before the fall of Saigon. In the letter, there were none of the secret codes or phrases he and Xuan had agreed to use should a disaster the magnitude of South Vietnam's surrender ever actually befall them when they were separated, and if Lynch was unable to rescue Xuan.

She was dead. Of that, he was now convinced.

Someone knocked on the door, and Lynch looked up, startled. His eyes scanned the light blue walls of the Officers Club rest room.

"Everything okay in there, Colonel?" a voice from outside called.

"Uh, yes . . . right—no problem," Lynch responded dryly.

"There's a car outside for you, sir," the youthful, energetic voice said. "It's waiting to take you to the shuttle simulator."

Lynch opened the door and stared down at the boyish, clean-shaven face of an eighteen- or nineteen-year-old SP. "Thanks, son."

"Sir?" the blue-bereted air cop asked him. "Is it true you're going to be on the next shuttle flight?"

"That's what they tell me," Lynch replied modestly.

"Well . . . would you mind if . . . if I got your autograph, sir?"

Lynch laughed, and reached for the pen. ''No sweat, son.'' Then he took the youth's logbook and scribbled his trademark signature across the inside cover.

''Good luck, Colonel.'' The SP saluted sharply as Lynch headed for a pay phone on the wall prior to leaving for his daily ten hours of astronaut refresher training.

''Thanks, son,'' he smiled grimly. ''I'm going to need it.''

Before leaving the Officers Club, Colonel Lynch needed to make calls to NASA Security, Air Force Intelligence and the Office of Special Investigations.

The deal with Yuri the Ogre was off.

15

The men of Able Team sat locked and loaded—buckled, actually—into their heavily padded launch survival modules. They stared at the backs of the helmets of the *Enterprise*'s primary flight crew: two colonels and a general, handpicked by NASA and the Pentagon. They had met the officers briefly during their recent rigorous training.

Lyons had recognized none of the men who had escorted the group from final-briefing bag to the heavily armed motorcade that had delivered them to the launch facilities.

They were now seated with their backs down—toward the earth, although the ground was several hundred feet below—and chests, knees and faces pointing up. Toward the stars. Facing their destiny.

Remote-control video cameras swung on mechanical arms from the padded arms of their launch chairs to a locked position several inches safely in front of their heads.

In the background, Mission Control was proceeding with the countdown. "T minus thirty seconds...twenty-nine...twenty-eight..."

Although they were busy with minor duties NASA had assigned them, the men of Able Team were nervous and jabbering away to each other on the private channel that supposedly could not be monitored by NASA technicians. They'd been in the military game long enough to know that *everything* was monitored, however.

It didn't seem to bother Blancanales. "Pinch me, Gadgets," he said, "so I'll know this all just isn't a wonderful dream."

"I would, if this space suit wasn't so damn bulky. I can't even—"

"It's real," Lyons told them. "Believe it."

"T minus twenty seconds...nineteen...eighteen..."

"At least you didn't have to fork over ten million for the chance to—"

"Quiet back there." The shuttle commander's voice seemed unusually calm—not tense or excited in the least.

"Yeah—" Gadgets tried not to nod, but the space helmet prevented much movement "—you guys knock off the chatter. I want to listen to NASA now. This is better than '*Star Trek*.'"

"Damn, but I wish I could see what's going on outside," Blancanales whispered.

No sooner had he voiced his desires than the video monitors, hanging suspended in front of the three short-notice astronauts, flickered on. They showed dual-screen views of the *Enterprise* from the ground observation bunkers, and, looking down from a camera positioned somewhere aboard the shuttle itself, shots of the surrounding terrain.

"T minus ten...nine...eight...seven..."

Blancanales ignored his cram-course training of the last week and found himself staring at the video monitors instead. Smoke was actually beginning to billow forth from below the giant liquid-fuel rocket they were strapped to.

"This is it," Lyons muttered under his breath. "Let's just shut up and do it."

"Five...four...three..."

Gadgets Schwarz stared at the monitor, eyes glued to the scene unfolding. He was actually becoming a part of history. His dream of accompanying a shuttle crew into Earth orbit was actually being realized! He had never imagined that duty with Able Team would lead to bennies as great as this!

"We have ignition," a voice at Mission Control droned with little emotion.

The USS *Enterprise* began to tremble and shudder. On the monitor, one half of the dual screen was zooming in on the thrust cowlings of the solid-fuel rocket boosters. Sparks and smoke were beginning to swirl.

"Two...one..."

A terrific roar came from below, and their headsets filled with the hundred jabbering voices of Mission Control. Carl Lyons realized his eyes were tightly closed, and he forced them open, willed them to stare out at the monitors.

A burst of thrust shook the orbiter, and monstrous flames poured out of the rocket booster's giant exhaust nozzles, but just as it seemed the craft was about to break the bonds of gravity, the flames suddenly died to a flickering glow.

The roller coaster ride had come to an abrupt stop—the *Enterprise* ceased vibrating.

"What the hell?"

Lyons concentrated on the words filling his headset. The men and women at Mission Control were still exchanging data with rapid-fire speed, as if the shuttle had actually cleared the ground.

"And we have lift-off," an excited voice was announcing, "at twenty-two-zero-seven hours...the space shuttle *Atlantis* has now cleared the launchpad..."

"What the *hell*? Did he say *Atlantis*?" Lyons asked as he reached forward and fiddled with the remote control until he had the on-board camera scan of the entire Cape Phoenix launch facilities. And that was when he saw her.

Rising from deep within the dreaded, off-limits HADES compound some two or three nautical miles to the east was another space shuttle: the USS *Atlantis*.

"Sorry, guys," one of the colonels said as he removed his flight helmet and glanced back over his shoulder with the most sheepish look Lyons had ever seen.

"What the hell is going on?" Blancanales demanded, removing his helmet as well. He was in no mood for mere apologies.

"We received word that the Soviets were getting desperate." The *Enterprise*'s commander detached himself from the safety harness and stood up on the access ramp protruding from one inner wall of the orbiter. "We were informed that they might go so far as to destroy the shuttle on the ground, rather than allow this phase of SDI experimentation to proceed."

"You mean—" Gadgets's jaw went slack "—we could have just been—"

"Most unceremoniously *zapped*," Blancanales whispered, "by a Commie laser orbiting in space?"

"But it didn't happen, did it?" the second colonel said as he, too, removed his flight helmet. "No Soviet laser beam destroyed us. We're all in one piece, although perhaps we're disappointed."

"I'd like to string Brognola up for this," Schwarz muttered.

"We're just soldiers—" Lyons shook his head in resignation "—with a mission to do—whatever that mission might be. We just follow orders, guys."

"You should be proud," the first colonel said. "You've just participated in the latest in a continuing series of solid-fuel booster tests. And it was a success! Now how many of your neighbors back home will be able to say they rode atop the shuttle during a controlled test of full thrust?''

"HADES," Lyons mumbled. "Toxic waste disposal, my ass."

"It's actually a giant, underground facility," the general revealed. "Makes Cape Phoenix look like a Little League baseball diamond. Basically we converted the floor of a huge box canyon to NASA use."

"They call it Cape Luna," one of the colonels laughed. "Because it resembles a monster crater on the moon. The entire facility remains covered most of the time by a gargantuan canopy constructed of the same materials they're using for the *Stealth* fighter bomber. The damn place is virtually undetectable by radar *and* recon satellite."

"That crazy Brognola," Schwarz sighed. "We were a diversion—nothing more than a damned decoy."

"Well, at least we didn't get blasted out of space by a Soviet laser," Pol rationalized as he began unfastening his own net of seat belts. "I hope the men aboard *Atlantis* are as lucky."

"Are you guys really astronauts?" Lyons asked the officers.

"I am," the first colonel admitted. "Here to coordinate the on-board computers and controls. They could have done it all by remote, of course, but I needed the hours. And the experience. I'm going to be aboard the *next* shuttle launch."

"We're antiespionage specialists with Air Force Intelligence," the other colonel said, gesturing toward the general. "No hard feelings?"

"No wonder Brognola was so low-key and unconcerned about our lack of experience," Schwarz said. "'You're just along for the ride, guys. You're just passengers.' Well, shee-it!"

"We weren't really going anywhere in the first place," Blancanales added.

"We were a decoy, dudes," Lyons repeated his earlier realization. "A diversion."

"We were expendable." Gadgets Schwarz voiced the opinion the other men of Able Team did not want to think about.

COLONEL PAUL LYNCH stared down at the dreamy image of planet Earth, from his window aboard the space shuttle *Atlantis*.

If only he didn't have to go back. If only things were different. He knew that they would find out. He knew his secret would be discovered.

"Quite a view, isn't it?" someone remarked, tapping him on the shoulder from behind. It was one of the men he'd attended refresher training with.

"Yes, a splendid view." He could just discern Vietnam's outline below the cloud cover of an approaching monsoon downpour.

Lynch did not like the man floating so close to him. They were experiencing weightless conditions now as *Atlantis* circled the Earth, and three of the other astronauts prepared Peg-7 for deployment.

The two men were supposed to be busy with a space medicine experiment. The other man had annoyed Lynch ever since he reported for duty at the refresher training course. Rory Calhoun was an Air Force officer whom Lynch had had the displeasure of first meeting in Vietnam. *North* Vietnam.

At the Hanoi Hilton.

Calhoun was one of the radical prisoners who'd been incarcerated in Room One of the "warehouse." Radical, as in antiwar and un-American, not pro-POW. And incarcerated, as in country club.

But all of that was in the past, according to the Air Force. No charges had ever been pressed against any U.S. prisoner of war held in North Vietnam. There had been "insufficient evidence." Besides, it was time to heal the wounds inflicted by Vietnam, time to bring the country back together again. Right?

And hadn't Calhoun—a big, broad-shouldered blonde with that certain air of leadership about him—distinguished himself highly during the past fifteen years? Advancing in rank to full-bird colonel, like Lynch himself. Despite the stigma, despite what the Communists had put them all through.

"If you don't mind...." Lynch's frown drove Calhoun away.

"Of course," he said, gruffly, eyes narrowing.

Lynch busied himself with his portion of the experiment, but always found his eyes returning to the thick glass windows for a peak at Earth and the spectacular, swirling solar system beyond.

After completing the complicated series of experiments, the colonel began his routine purge of duplicate data from the ship's computers, as well as the hourly scan of incoming research information from sensitive instruments mounted outside the orbiter.

A shiver raced down his spine when he deciphered the latest information: the *Atlantis*'s guidance program had been tampered with sometime *after* launch. And by someone *on board*. Lynch's attention automatically shifted to Calhoun, who was watching him from a position near the cargo-bay bulkhead.

Lynch dug deeper through the computer programs and found that the hydraulic power needed to lift Peg-7 out of the cargo bay, and to later retrieve the Soviet nuclear reactor, had been directed to malfunction halfway through the necessary maneuvers.

Lynch corrected the problems by quietly feeding a delete-and-reset program into the system. Then, when the other astronauts were busy preparing to initiate Project Pegasus, the colonel dispatched a coded message to Mission Control, with a Priority One Divert to Air Force Intelligence. The message read:

Atlantis has been sabotaged. You will find a satellite relay switching device on the grounds of Vandenberg, in the cliffs overlooking Capes Phoenix and Luna. The device must be destroyed immediately, or this mission is doomed: the *Atlantis* will crash on reentry, and the resulting dispersion of radioactive materials from *Cosmos* 1900 will be catastrophic.

Lynch then fed the approximate ground location of Skylink into the transmitter. But before he could warn search teams on the ground that the device was booby-trapped to prevent tampering or removal, a shadow fell over his console, and the microwave feed was suddenly shut down.

"Very poor judgment call, comrade," Calhoun whispered into his ear. "We cannot allow Project Pegasus to succeed. It would tip the balance of power in favor of the world's oppressors: America. You are making my job very difficult."

"I always suspected that you were the traitor, Calhoun," Lynch said as he started to stand. "I demanded many times that the chief of staff nail you to a cross and—"

"*You* are the one who is doomed here today," Calhoun said, bringing a wrench down hard across Lynch's forehead. "Not this mission."

His skull fractured, Hawkjaw Lynch collapsed across his console, spreading rivulets of crimson over its blinking lights.

Calhoun then produced a cutting device as the other astronauts—their attention centered on preparing Peg-7 for deployment—opened the cargo-bay doors.

The curved ceiling of *Atlantis* split apart to reveal a brilliant panorama of endless galaxies that seemed close enough to touch, although they were light-years away.

Paying little notice to the spectacular scene unfolding nearby, Calhoun snipped Lynch's oxygen and life-support lines. He dragged him by the arms, backing toward the bulkhead that separated the command bridge from the much larger cargo section of the craft. His intent was to hurl Lynch's body out into space, then take the other astronauts hostage until he succeeded in sabotaging Peg-7.

As skilled as the KGB had made him, Calhoun had been unable to smuggle a firearm aboard the *Atlantis*. A gun's discharge aboard the orbiter would probably mean instant death for everyone, in any case. But there were other weapons around, just as lethal—one merely had to identify them and use them to one's advantage. He was the biggest man aboard the space shuttle and would also use his sheer size to intimidate the others if it came down to that.

Calhoun had a mission: Project Pegasus must not succeed. He would destroy the *Atlantis*, if he had to, in attempting to reach that goal.

The former-POW-turn-Communist-sympathizer's plans went astray, however, the moment he reached the bulkhead passageway.

"Hold it right there, asshole. Drop the wrench and release the colonel, or you're going to be the next supernova to blow up in outer space—after I fill you with black holes. And that's no hollow, Moscow-made promise. That's *fact*."

Calhoun turned to find Captain Nacy Lourdes, rookie astronaut and veteran counterterrorist SP, standing inside the cargo-bay passageway, blocking his path with a Taser electric-shock dart gun.

16

"I certainly could do without these short-notice missions, Gadgets!" Pol Blancanales complained as he slammed the seven-round magazine into his .45's hollow handle with a dull but powerful thud.

Beside him, Lyons fed a speed-loader, containing six 158-grain hollowpoints into the open cylinder of his .357 Magnum. "Ain't *that* the sticky truth!" Ironman agreed, slapping the revolver's cylinder shut and running his meaty fingers along the blue-steel barrel. "Never a vacation I can truly call my own. And I can practically see the roller coaster at Disneyland. Ain't no justice in this city without pity. Hell, I can just about hear Mickey Mouse calling for Annette Funicello from here," he added, still refusing to smile.

"Just about." Blancanales nodded somberly. Disneyland was actually some hundred and fifty miles away. And the closest thing to Mickey's ears was the two-disk communications dish mounted atop one of the air base guard towers nearby.

"Hey, it's not my fault the Chief decided to keep us working on this screwup instead of calling in the cavalry—you clowns should be flattered." Hermann Schwarz stared at Rosario's sinister-looking automatic. "What's the matter? You afraid we won't be able to locate and waste those KGB wimps most expeditiously?"

Blancanales ran his palm along the .45's barrel—
smooth with a thin layer of LSA gun oil across it now—
and suddenly jerked back on the slide, chambering a
round. "We aren't afraid of shit, amigo," he snarled at
Gadgets, flipping the safety up with his right thumb. The
modified colt was built around the classic M-1911A1
frame and now included such refinements as Parkerized
black finish, blunt suppressor, fold-down lever, enlarged
trigger guard, and phosphorous sights. The added features helped make a good weapon great. In Blancanales's
massive fist, the .45 almost looked tiny, however.

Gadgets glanced back at Lyons again. His brown eyes
locked on to Ironman's icy blue orbs, then dropped to the
Python's magnaported, 152 mm barrel. Blancanales
stared back at him with an equally grim determination
creasing his dark features. Both warriors looked as lean
and mean as he had ever seen them in the past. They
looked hungry. Hungry for the change to confront Lady
Death, taunt her with the Big Sleep, and pull a deadly
swindle in the end.

His eyes shifted to Pol's again. Inky, bottomless pits,
concealing the ex-Black Beret's next move. Schwarz's own
sixth sense told him the Politician was anxious to pounce.
And when the proper time came, Lyons would back
Rosario up, in true ex-cop fashion. No doubt about it.
This was not exactly the reunion he'd envisioned only a
short week or so ago, while jogging along Goldenwest
Boulevard on the outskirts of Little Saigon. Able Team
was back on the street again, headed for the eye of the
storm—not the carefree reunion of drinking binges, floor-
show critiques and fox-trot contests he'd imagined before
being "kidnapped" by Reilly's Air Force commandos the
week before.

"Gadgets, you've definitely made my current shit list,"
Ironman said, grabbing the front of his shirt as well as his
attention. Lyons suddenly looked bigger than his actual

six foot two and two hundred pounds. He pulled Gadgets closer, until they were nearly nose-to-nose.

"Yep, you have truly made Ironman's shit list," Blancanales confirmed, sweeping his hair off his forehead as the heat inside the parked van started to rise.

Schwarz's meek reply was to swallow loudly, and the resulting croaking sound filled the cramped quarters. The noise brought instant and involuntary smiles to the two men confronting him. As Ironman continued to clasp the front of Gadgets's shirt, Pol reached up and gently slapped the back of the electronics genius's head. "You and your penchant for science projects and space probes!" Blancanales chuckled. "*That's* what got us into this Vandenberg fiasco. I hope you're happy!"

"Yeah!" taunted Lyons. "We *should* be sunning our buns on some white sand beach in Hawaii right about now, taking a break from the 'war.' But nooooo! Gadgets has to go and get us entwined in another no-win situation."

"The no-good lowlife almost got our butts flung into low Earth orbit." Blancanales chuckled a bit louder this time.

Carl Lyons erupted into hearty laughter as well. He thrust Schwarz back against the opposite wall of the van, and the chassis rocked back and forth from the powerful impact. "Sure is good to be back on solid ground, ain't it, brother?"

The Politician nodded in total agreement. "In one *piece*!"

Schwarz's eyes darted back and forth between the two vets. They had been squeezing his brain again. Twisting his head without leaving any marks. "Well, hell!" Gadgets complained as he expanded his chest importantly. "You jerkettes scared the shit out of me! I mean, I thought you were going to blame *me* for this whole mess.

I just happened to be in the wrong place at the wrong time, you know!''

"You know we love you like a mother!" Blancanales embraced Schwarz in an unwanted bear hug, then roughly pushed him away—into the wall of the van again.

"Well, let's get on with the mission, then," Lyons ordered, a businesslike look glazing his eyes once more. He turned his back on them as he cautiously lifted the shades covering the Air Force van's rear window and peered out.

But Ironman's grin remained intact. It *was* good to have Able Team back on solid ground. Accompanying astronauts into space would have been a once-in-a-lifetime opportunity, true—but one he'd just as soon do without. Lyons satisfied his lust for excitement and adventure by chasing after low-life hooligans and back-alley denizens of the urban underworld—on street level. He didn't need to be thrust into low Earth orbit to start the adrenaline rush flowing.

But viewing America, Homeland of the Free and the Brave, from outer space *would* have been grand....

No time to muse about that now, though, he thought. Brognola wanted them back out on the bricks, combing the town for a group of Soviet agents that was supposedly threatening the real orbiter mission.

The KGB would be on the lookout for FBI and even CIA operatives. Brognola—and the President—felt that only Able Team stood a chance of rounding up the Communists before they made any further attempts at blocking the successful completion of the USS *Atlantis*'s geostationary mission.

And the President's faith in "that Stony Man bunch" was well founded. Able Team had distinguished itself in concrete jungles from New York to Miami to San Francisco, a dozen times over. They had yet to lose a major skirmish in the running gun battle against evil. Their existence was blatant proof of that.

Blancanales seemed to read the look of disappointment that lingered in Schwarz's eyes. "Hang in there," he told the amateur scientist. "Before you know it, every Joe Blow and Jane Doe on the planet will be able to buy a ticket for a thrill ride aboard the orbiter. We'll be the first trio of madmen in line when that day arrives, pal."

Gadgets was trying to ignore his friend's display of affection when the driver's side door popped open. As three gun hands instinctively went to holstered pistol butts, a young woman wearing cammie fatigues and a blue security police beret jumped in behind the steering wheel. Recognizing Pamela Pearce, Able Team relaxed.

"How's it hanging?" Pol grinned.

"It's going down," she announced with jaw muscles twitching, which automatically increased the tension level inside the van's cramped, stuffy quarters. "Sergeant Tuskin advised me to have you deployed along the northern perimeter. We can insert you just a couple of hundred yards down from the main gate on that side without being observed."

"Just exactly *what's* going down?" Blancanales shouted.

"Our eye in the sky has spotted a small force moving toward the northwest perimeter coastline. Frogmen aboard two rubber rafts. Heavily armed."

"Why are they coming ashore at high noon?" Schwarz asked, turning to face Lyons. "Frogmen with any bush sense would wait until after dark, don't you think?"

"Unless they've been watching—and I'm sure they have," Blancanales cut in, "and they know how heavily guarded this place is at night. Once the sun comes up, however, security is slashed nearly in half. Maybe that's why they're making their move now." His mind played back an aerial tour of Vandenberg's missile test site: miles and miles of endless perimeter fence line in three stages, across the barren dry lake bed. Two distinctly separate compounds within the three rings of chain-link and barbed wire. Vandenberg's administration buildings and aerospace lab facilities, and the space shuttle launch complex were both located near the southern perimeter border. Guard towers overlooked the two primary compounds, but not the entire perimeter—monitoring the vast fence line was the responsibility of roving patrols.

"And is Air Force Intelligence sure they're not just some of our Navy Seals trying to make your SPs look bad?" Lyons asked as his hands moved swiftly, readying his gear, despite the skepticism in his voice.

"They're KGB to the core," Pearce said grimly as she stared straight ahead and popped the clutch.

The van lurched forward and started down the narrow, winding road. "Four men per raft. Eight total. Armed with shortbarreled, small-stock weapons of some sort. Probably Uzis. Think you bad boys can handle them?"

"We can handle them," Schwarz responded without emotion.

"What kind of backup do you have for us?" Ironman asked, although he didn't really sound like he needed any.

"Two Reactionary Alert Teams are waiting at the SP barracks, in full combat gear."

"That's too far away," Blancanales said, his voice taking on an almost comical quality because of the road bumps Pearce seemed to be going out of her way to hit. The van bounced about like an M-60 tank through a battlefield pockmarked with foxholes.

"They're waiting aboard helicopter gunships," she explained. "Ready to respond the instant you call for help."

"That makes a difference," Ironman argued, nodding to Pol as he holstered his revolver.

"I want you to know I think this is a bad idea," Pearce revealed suddenly. She monitored their movements by keeping one eye on the mirror at all times as she negotiated the poorly maintained perimeter road. "It was an Air

Force matter in the beginning, and it should have *stayed* an Air Force matter all along. We're professionally trained, you know. Just like regular civilian police officers. And like I just explained, we've even got a full-fledged combat detachment. Our people can handle just about anything that could possible come up and—''

"The Air Force obviously wants to keep the SPs out of this one," Lyons snapped. "For the most part."

"What?" Pearce's eyes narrowed at the news. Nobody had briefed her on *this* development.

"The SPs are highly skilled and fairly modernized," Schwarz said, raising his voice against the van's engine roar as it strained to pull them up over a steep hill without losing speed. "We'll grant you that. But let's face it: this is the boonies. Your people are still using some antiquated communications equipment. Most of the bands and frequencies are monitored by the civilian press in Lompoc and surrounding communities."

"You're right." Pearce gnawed at her lower lip. "So what's your point?"

"We don't require fancy communications," Blancanales told her. "Only each other."

"We'll cancel the bad guys' tickets without making a public stink about it," Schwarz added. "And two-on-one odds ain't too shabby. If we can neutralize that team of KGB sappers without the press corps learning about it, then so much the better."

Pearce glanced back over a shoulder as they started down a gentle straightaway. "I calculate it to be more like three to one odds, gentlemen."

"We'll take that," Schwarz said quickly. "It could be a lot worse. It's certainly *been* a lot worse in the past."

"They've probably got a damn submarine sitting out there beyond the coral reef," Blancanales muttered, grabbing on to a handhold as they bounced across a rough section of the perimeter.

"I think we should pull back, lay low and radio for reinforcements," Sergeant Pearce said. "You guys don't have to risk life and limb just to impress little old *me*!"

"Have some faith, girl," Blancanales returned. "Your people are good, but they wouldn't get to first base playing hardball with these KGB goons. They'd just get dead."

"Rather impressed with yourself, aren't you?" Pearce said, directing a smirk at the Politician as they briefly locked eyes in the rearview mirror.

"Just drive," Ironman ordered. "And leave the fireworks to friends."

He slammed a swollen aluminum briefcase down against the van's floorboards. The black case was equipped with two combination locks, but was apparently not sealed. Lyons flipped the hinges open and three Car-15 assault rifles—cut-down versions of the mainstay M-16—came into view. They were broken down behind the handguards, and held securely inside the case with Velcro straps.

Lyons quickly freed the first weapon, said, "Dig in!" and began assembling the two halves. In less than thirty seconds, he had the ammo magazine sliding into the weapon's bottom clip receptacle and was switching the fire selector to full-auto.

Pearce's eyes did a double take, widening slightly. Capable of delivering 750-round bursts of 5.56 mm destruction, the Car-15 was vastly superior to the Uzi's 9 mm in terms of muzzle velocity, range and foot-pounds of energy. It had been designed to meet a request by American soldiers serving in Vietnam, who needed a smaller version of their issue M-16A1 when engaged in close-quarters combat.

Military designers reduced the length of the M-16's barrel to 9.9 inches, which in turn produced a much larger muzzle-flash—a problem that was offset by equipping the carbine with a bigger flash suppressor. The basic mechanics of the M-16 were not altered—the seven to eight hundred rounds per minute rate of fire remained. And the gas-operated Colt Commando—as it was more affectionately known by the Army brass—featured selective fire and a holding-open device, which considerably reduced the ammo jams that could mean a death sentence in the rain forest courtrooms of Indochina. The Colt Commando quickly proved to be such a popular weapon among infantrymen that it became one of the primary-issue firearms of the elite Special Forces—the Green Berets. With sling attached and thirty-round clip inserted, the Colt Commando weighed in at just slightly over an easily manageable seven pounds.

Gadgets Schwarz tensed as they approached the final curve in the launch site's northeast perimeter. The target group was still four or five miles away—somewhere along the northwest quadrants that bordered the sea, but already he could feel the adrenaline rush preparing him to fight.

"Lock and load," Lyons announced unnecessarily as the vast blue expanse of Pacific Ocean suddenly came into view. His eyes shifted to the van's speedometer. Pearce was keeping the dial between ninety and a hundred.

"Damn!" Blancanales pounded his fist against the van's side panel. "There they are.

The van's four occupants could clearly see the black outline of their wetsuit-clad opponents against the slowly shifting heat waves. The frogmen had advanced nearly two kilometers across the rolling hills overlooking the beach, and were brazenly trotting along the perimeter roadway itself, swimming masks and flippers removed and buried, no doubt, but body rubber and cold-steel firepower remaining.

There were no guard towers along this outer fence line, only roving SP trucks that crisscrossed the property twice every half hour or so. Today they had been conveniently called back and quartered by Major Fletcher, on orders from Hal Brognola.

"No time to ditch this van and sneak up on the bastards as we had hoped," Lyons decided. He could smell smoke on the air, and envisioned shoulder-launched, heat-seeking missiles soaring up through the drifting haze toward the approaching orbiter, but he knew the odor probably came from the overused van's exhaust system.

His sharp eyes locked on to the approaching Communist sappers. It was not that often Able Team was actually unleashed on hard-core field elements of the KGB's insurgency brigade. Ironman was looking forward to the confrontation. He was going to relish it. More than a pop quiz, it would be a death test of his—and Able Team's—skills.

The next few minutes would not be an easy, quick kill, however. Brognola's instructions had been very clear, unfortunately: isolate, neutralize and bring in as many survivors as possible—for questioning.

Prisoners. Lyons hated taking prisoners, but he knew it was a necessary evil, if secrets were to be learned, and the long-range battles were to be won.

And then an obstacle appeared at the bottom of the hill.

At first Lyons leaned forward when he saw the frogmen darting to the side of the roadway and disappearing into a field of thick foliage. But then he quickly saw the reason for the abrupt diversion: coming around a bend in the roadway was a group of thirty or forty airmen. Clad only in running shorts and tennis shoes, they were covered in thin, glistening layers of perspiration as they jogged around the perimeter, singing cadences about the "wild blue yonder."

They were also unarmed.

17

"What the hell?" Schwarz demanded. "Didn't those guys get the word?"

Pearce popped her bubble gum loudly. "The notorious Air Force bureaucracy breaks down again," she said without visible emotion.

"Shit," Lyons said, his eyes bulging until it appeared they might explode as he contemplated alternate plans of action. "We've got to get those men out of there."

"The Commies have seen our van by now," Blancanales nodded. "They know something's up."

"Floor your gas pedal," Lyons told Pearce. "And hit your horn."

"Then what?" she asked as she immediately complied.

"The airmen haven't seen the Commies yet. We drive right down through the middle of the flyboys' jogging formation and spread 'em apart, forcing them to take cover in the barrow pits along the side of the road. Then, after you get past the last runner, fishtail this baby to the right. I want to come down hard, right on top of those frogmen, muzzles blazing. I don't want to give them a chance to figure out what's happening."

"Just don't hit any of the airmen," Schwarz cautioned.

"Hey, cut me some slack, okay? I'm not a rookie!" Pearce snapped indignantly. "I could take this crate to the

Indy 500 and rate an honorable mention, minimum, mister!"

Shrugging, Schwarz did not apologize. He was too busy double-checking his rifle's thirty-round banana clips. He always kept two taped together, business ends opposite, so that when one clip ran out of bullets, all he needed to do was eject it, flip it over, and another thirty rounds presented themselves for rapid-fire distribution.

In the rearview mirror, Pearce watched him slap the palm of his hand again the ammo magazine's bottom, ensuring a tight seal with the rifle's feeder well.

"If you can see past the dust cloud after we spin out," Blancanales told her, "make sure you get word to any airmen who aren't already kissing dirt to keep their heads down. We don't want any innocents getting caught in the cross fire."

"They can take care of themselves," the female sergeant grinned, reaching back behind her seat to pull a shotgun out from its concealed hiding place. "Pam Pearce turns Athena today," she said. "*I'm* your backup, boys...."

In a one-handed, jerking motion, she dramatically pumped a round into the weapon's chamber. "Gadgets loaned this hummer to me. 'Just...in...case'—*his* words." Her lips stretched into a wide grin.

"Holy Smoker," Schwarz exclaimed. The outburst seemed a bit contrived to Ironman, as if he was auditioning for the part of Robin in a Batman movie.

Lyons shook his head from side-to-side. "That's *my* Atchisson!" He glared over at Schwarz, who glanced away sheepishly.

The Atchisson Assault 12 was a sleek and beautiful example of gunsmithing and weaponscraft at its finest. An automatic, 12-bore shotgun similar to the fancy assault rifles now on the market, it was even deadlier when loaded with 12-gauge shells that packed one hell of a punch after travelling 366 meters per second to their target. Finding oneself on the business end of an Atchisson was like being shot point-blank by a firing squad of fifty men, all armed with .32-caliber pistols.

Sergeant Pearce glanced into the mirror one final time as they approached what would have to double as the drop-off zone: the shoulder of the road amid the group of startled airmen who were already scattering as the blue Air Force van raced toward them. She gently shook her head in amazement as she scanned the faces of Lyons, Blancanales and Schwarz. It was hard to believe they were actually working with the full sanction of General Farthing. It was, in fact, incredible!

Though it was early afternoon, the men of Able Team wore night camouflage gear. Initially they had expected a daylight insertion, with prolonged predusk field observation most likely culminating in an after-dark firefight when enemy sappers were finally detected.

That the frogmen chose to come ashore now was unexpected but not something that the team would be unable to deal with on such short notice. Able Team was, after all, as much an emergency response squad as any urban SWAT unit. In fact, Lyons and the others were always expecting the best-laid plans to go awry—for they usually did. And today their equipment showed it: beneath the nightsuits were Kevlar bullet-proof body armor. Various pyrotechnic devices, ranging from fragmentation grenades to small tear-gas cannisters, adorned their jet-black web gear. Seven-inch daggers were strapped to their thighs as an additional tool for survival if events deteriorated to hand-to-hand combat.

"Good luck," Pearce said, forcing the words out as her hands guided the van between the parting waves of cursing joggers. Trailing the expected cloud of dust, the van's motor roared as Pearce downshifted, and then she jerked the sheering wheel hard to the right, bringing the vehicle into a wild fishtail. More dust billowed forth, creating a virtual smoke screen as she pulled over to the side of the road. "This *is* the place: all ashore who's going ashore!"

Silence was Able Team's response. Grim-faced silence, punctuated by thumbs-up gestures from Gadgets and Politician. And then the back doors flew open, and they vanished in the cloud of rolling dust as it caught up to and enveloped the van.

THE KGB AGENTS were waiting for Able Team directly on the other side of the hill. Proned in the dry salt lake bed between sparse shrubs of scrub oak and cacti, the group's leader leveled a silent, accusing finger at Lyons and his men as they burst over the hilltop, Car-15s blazing.

Able Team was not aiming for flesh, however—not just yet. One of their favorite assault tactics involved firing into the ground a few feet in front of a dug-in or spread-eagled opponent. Opponents they wanted to capture alive. On blacktop or pavement, the ricocheting bullets would bounce low regardless of weapon angle, rarely rising eight or nine inches above the earth as they travelled on spent energy, burning off inertia and momentum. This property of ballistics and gravity almost always guaranteed head hits to any enemy gunman lying proned in the distance. Their current battlefield being a dust-covered dry lake bed of crushed salt, however, meant that the bullets would be absorbed by the earth instead of recklessly ricocheting.

Dust and stinging particles of salt swirled up like tiny whirlwinds, effectively blinding the Soviet agents as Able Team rushed their position.

"Get them!" the obvious leader among the frogmen—the man who had pointed at the charging Americans—now yelled in Russian.

Pol Blancanales raised his Car-15 barrel into the air and fired off another short burst. "Drop your weapons!" He was not quite screaming, yet his deep voice carried well beyond the farthest low-crawling Russian.

Few of the KGB agents actually complied, but like a sea of minnows parting for three sharks, they broke apart, rolling to the sides as Able Team advanced.

With lightninglike efficiency and a profound sense of confidence, Ironman took the lead. With his gun hand, he waved Schwarz around to the right. All three of the American commandos immediately assessed the potential retaliatory capabilities of the enemy, then chose targets of opportunity: the front line of four frogmen, who all brandished AKMS assault rifles, and not Uzis.

The AKMS was an ultramodern version of the more recognizable AK-47. Equipped with a folding stock for easy concealment, the Soviet machine gun spat 7.62 mm death in indiscriminant bursts.

A big man in his late forties with thick eyebrows appeared in the forefront of all the action. He brought up his weapon, but hesitated pulling the trigger for some reason.

With his free hand, Lyons waved Pol around to the left.

Blancanales's nod was the only acknowledgement necessary—the giant was all his. In a smooth, fluid motion, Pol slipped his Car-15's sling over his head, allowing the assault rifle to flop diagonally across his back, the barrel pointing toward the ground. It was time to take prisoners.

Colt .45 extended at arm's length now, Pol sprinted toward the stocky Russian, who finally sent a burst from his AK in the direction of the unarmed airmen who had begun appearing along the crest of the hill like curious spectators. The initial series of discharges had not sent them running for long. Firearms were their business, and these off-duty SPs—although unarmed—were not intimidated. They dropped into cautious crouches behind a jutting hedgerow as the eight or nine slugs of lead fell short, kicking up dust and salt a dozen feet down the hillside from their position.

"I said *drop it*!" Ironman commanded a second and last time. As soon as his eyes locked with the Soviet's, he received his answer. There was no alternative, and Lyons smoothly pulled on the trigger at the same moment the Politician's Colt .45 began barking off to the side.

Their dual bursts of lead smoked in a precise swath across the ground in front of the frogmen. And then Ironman's rifle jerked up a foot or two and he sent a single, soft-nosed slug out to ruin the big sapper's day.

The Soviet plopped back out of sight—a crimson spray floating in the air where his forehead had been only an instant before. The blood sprinkled down across the dry lake bed's salt-white surface.

Barrels waving side to side like angry serpents guarding their eggs, two AKs exploded from the front ranks of the frogmen and, from off to the side, Schwarz unleashed several short bursts with his cut-down carbine. He silenced four of the Soviets as the bullets drilled a lethal trench across shocked East-Bloc faces, left to right, and swiftly back again.

Ignoring the obvious threat that still existed from the three surviving sappers, the Politician dropped to one knee as he changed the taped ammo magazines—ejecting the banana clip and flipping it over.

"Ironman!" Blancanales yelled above the frenzy of echoing discharges bouncing back at them from the surrounding low-lying hills. "I had the sucker dead to rights, you shameless turkey!"

"Then drop the hammer on his boyfriends!" Gadgets shouted, pointing at the three men who were finally rising from behind mounds of salt and windswept sand. The surviving Communists were very young and looked like unwilling recruits forced into their first cross-border Lurp recon. Lyons could not believe the Kremlin would send such green youngsters into the hell of combat. But, of course, there *was* only one way to obtain that much-coveted experience. It required leaping into the fire, jumping boots first.

Having overcome the initial fear and panic at having lost their leader so quickly, the youths knew that surrender would not be condoned by their superiors back in the U.S.S.R. What they lacked in experience, they made up for in courage, however. All three unleashed short, deadly bursts from their AKs, apparently bent on not going down without a fight.

"Damn!" Lyons muttered as his Car-15 jammed on a defective cartridge. With the palm of his hand, he slammed the ejector port several times, but the shell refused to budge—it appeared to have warped immediately after discharge, effectively blocking the breech.

He reached down and drew his commando knife, well aware there would not be enough time to force the cartridge free with the blade's tip. His two partners were ramming home fresh ammo clips, but they would not be fast enough, either.

This was it. This was doomsday for Able Team. Or so it seemed.

Deafening discharges behind the three Americans proved the Ironman wrong—and it was an argument with destiny he did not mind losing.

Sergeant Pamela Pearce appeared on the hilltop a few dozen feet behind the commandos from Stony Man Farm. Blasting away with her shotgun as she sauntered down through the cacti and scrub oak, the security policewoman let out an uncharacteristic war cry as she unleashed nearly a half dozen rounds of explosive buckshot into the ranks of the three surviving Soviets.

Pearce's aim was extraordinary, especially given the type of weapon she had to work with and the considerable range involved. She decapitated two of the three targets from twenty meters.

"Holy Mary!" Blancanales exclaimed, slowly lowering the rifle that he'd just brought to his shoulder. He watched the two faceless skulls bounce down onto the dry lake bed and tumble out of sight between clumps of bright green flora. A huge bluish-green lizard burst from the foliage and scampered off on its hind legs in terror. A flock of turtle doves took to the air nearby—their wings exploding forth like a muffled Claymore blast—and every combatant still standing and able to breathe dropped into a low crouch or prone position, startled by the out-of-sync disturbance.

"Hold your fire!" Lyons yelled at Pearce as she continued shooting into the squad of Communist agents. The third youngster had sustained serious chest injuries from two blasts, but might live. "I want a prisoner out of this mess!"

Sergeant Pam Pearce stopped in her tracks, as if Ironman's words had been a slap that drew her from some emotional trance. Breathing in deeply, she savored the stench of cordite and gun smoke on the air. It lined her throat and tasted like black licorice.

Her chest heaving from the excitement and danger of the brief firefight, Pearce lifted her Atchisson Automatic above her head with one arm and let out another war cry, unaware that tears of relief were streaming down her cheeks.

Behind the long-haired SP, several dozen airmen in jogging shorts burst forth with cheers and wild applause at Pearce's performance.

Tech Sergeant Kip Tuskin lead the Air Force cheering section.

18

"They got it!"

"Well, all right!"

The three men were huddled around a closed-circuit TV screen, watching pictures from outer space: the USS *Atlantis* and her crew, orbiting Earth. The crew had just wrapped remote-control cables around the out-of-control Russian *Cosmos* 1900 nuclear satellite, and were reeling it back in through the open bay doors—a mere six hours after deploying Peg-7 and America's latest phase of SDI working technology over the equator.

"What a catch!"

"Moscow's going to have a cow over this, brothers!"

"Hell, the Soviets are lucky we were nice enough to snatch that nasty babe before it came down somewhere and hurled radioactive scrap metal all over the place."

"Tell that to Tass."

Inside the civilian minivan parked behind the Security Police headquarters at Vandenberg Air Force Base, Gadgets Schwarz leaned over the shoulders of Jack Grimaldi and Aaron "the Bear" Kurtzman. He stared down at the dual computer consoles the two men were working on. They used the screens—and the endless array of sophisticated equipment built into the van's reinforced walls behind them—to display constantly changing data and information from the numerous Southern California law enforcement agencies patrolling real estate within a hundred miles of NASA's new West Coast Launch facilities.

"Any word on the character the Chief told us to keep our eyes open for?" Schwarz asked, tapping a rigid forefinger against the black-and-white mug shot of Yuri Ogorodnikova.

"Only that his presence in the area has been verified by the regional FBI offices in both San Jose and San Francisco," Kurtzman mumbled as he switched frequencies from that of the California Highway Patrol to Lompoc PD.

Grimaldi laughed. "The Feds are a tad upset over all the mysterious questions we fed them through the wire regarding this Yuri character. They want to know what we have."

"What'd you tell them?" Schwarz asked as he leaned against the Bear's wheelchair and began fiddling with a squelch dial.

"Don't touch that!" Kurtzman slapped Gadgets's wrist with a sharp-edged ruler, then resumed triangulating suspected transmission points on a large tabletop acetate map.

Grimaldi laughed again. "We told them it was secret shit that required a Q-clearance. I think that really blew their minds."

"I don't believe many FBI agents on the West Coast carry a Q-clearance, unless they're investigating industrial espionage at some of the aerospace firms," Schwarz said seriously.

"Whatever." Kurtzman was immersed in his work, and doing his best to ignore the unwanted intrusion.

"Did you clowns get anything out of that KGB kid you picked up out on the perimeter this afternoon?" Grimaldi asked, a slight sparkle dancing in his eyes. He'd paid his dues in Southeast Asia, earning an Airmen's Medal, two Purple Hearts and more than a few ArComs as an Army pilot. He remained a crack jet jockey to this day, capable of handling virtually any sort of aircraft for the men of Stony Man Farm.

"He's singin' like a canary," Gadgets smiled proudly.

"Scopolamine?" The Bear glanced up willingly for the first time, curiosity gleaming in his own eyes.

"Hell if I know," Schwarz scratched at the stubble on his chin. "The Chief's handling the session of truth or consequences personally. Probably a combination of seconal and Quaaludes, if I know Brognola."

"Originally a knock-out combo," Kurtzman told them as he seemed to reflect on something. "Produces a zombielike stupor. Better than scopolamine, in my opinion. I guess they both have their bennies, however."

"And their drawbacks," Gadgets frowned. He hated all talk of drugs—even casual references made in the course of executing their duties. "Anyway, the surviving Soviet puke dropped his defenses pronto. Revealed that his comrades were actually Russian military, with some KGB background. We're beginning to think they were Spetsnaz."

"Soviet Special Forces?" Grimaldi cocked an eyebrow as anger flashed across his face.

"Roger that. They intended to dig in for the day, and penetrate the airfield, then Vandenberg compound after nightfall, eventually assaulting the security police headquarters itself."

"The SP headquarters?" Grimaldi's eyes opened wide. "What the hell for?"

"The KGB kid doesn't know—claims only his leader was privy to that little tidbit of info. And honcho-san has been reduced to maggot meat right now—food for the worms."

"A suicide squad, you think?" Grimaldi lifted a pencil from the computer console and began chewing on the eraser.

"Your guess is as good as mine," Schwarz said as he started to fiddle with another dial. Kurtzman ignored him this time. "But I doubt it. Spetsnaz usually don't work that way. They're not Iranian zealots, you know. They're professionals. We just happened to luck out and bang heads with the bastards. They must have figured it would be easy going so long as it was daylight and security was lax."

"And no press people latched on to this thing?" Kurtzman asked locking eyes with the electronics wizard.

"That's a big negative, Bear," Gadgets's smile broadened proudly.

"Do you think they came in via submarine?" Grimaldi asked. "I mean, could there possibly still be some nuke-heavy sub waiting out there off the coast?"

"It's possible," Schwarz shrugged. "but they weren't carrying any portable radios. If a sub *is* submerged out there in the big deep blue somewhere, they must have agreed on a prearranged rendezvous and extraction time. We've got sub-hunter planes crisscrossing the coastline with a vengeance right now, but nothing's turned up so far."

A new voice broke the short silence that followed. The minivan tilted slightly to one side then leveled out again as Lyons clambered up the side steps. "When'd you guys fly in?" His question was directed at Jack Grimaldi.

"This morning," the pilot replied.

"On Hal's orders?"

"Roger that. Took the Corsair," Grimaldi announced with a smile. The Cessna 425 turboprop was his favorite. "That C-12 piece of junk is down for repairs again—bullet-hole patches, actually."

"Don't tell me you sabotaged it yourself—" Kurtzman shook a fist at Grimaldi in mock rebuke "—or did you forget to unload your *pistola* before playing quick-draw with Brognola?"

"Don't you two start," Lyons warned with a lack of enthusiasm. He enjoyed having the two men from Stony Man aboard, but they could be an abrasive duo up close.

Aaron "the Bear" Kurtzman lived on second-floor quarters back at the farm, and was the group's resident computer fanatic and ace communications specialist. His duties included monitoring the output of local law enforcement agencies during missions. He succeeded at his job through an uncanny, almost spooky ability to tap in to the transmissions of anyone from truckers with CB radios, to state troopers setting up a radar trap down the road on the local highway band, to government intelligence forces using the most sophisticated computer and microwave technologies. As Lyons often wisecracked, even "Big Brother" would have a hard time hiding secret radio transmissions or scrambling confidential codes if the Bear was determined to intercept and interpret them.

Confined to a wheelchair since being paralyzed from the waist down during a siege that had occurred on the grounds of the Stony Man compound several years earlier, the Bear nevertheless began every morning with a half hour of stretching exercises and weight training. The program was designed to strengthen his upper body.

Although he had always conducted these exercise sessions in his quarters—known affectionately as "Bear's Lair" to the rest of the troops—Able Team had recently won a wager with Hal Brognola and the President himself...a bet that had nearly turned deadly. At mission's end, the group became the recipients of a fully equipped gymnasium to be built on the compound grounds.

Now the Bear exercised in slightly more luxurious surroundings.

Jack Grimaldi, on the other hand, was not only blessed with the use of all his limbs, but often thought he also possessed wings. The man lived for flying. In recent years—after successfully untangling himself from the web of Mafia influence and control—he'd taken to working for Stony Man. Grimaldi now flew the commandos into and out of hot spots. His past mob ties aside, Grimaldi was now considered a loyal teammate to Lyons and the others. They were tight as blood brothers, dedicated to the death.

"Where's Blancanales?" Grimaldi asked, glancing over Lyons's shoulder.

"Out in the sticks," Ironman responded with visible concern. "Looking for the Ogre."

"Alone?" It was Bear who showed some worry now.

"He'll be all right," Schwarz snickered. "He's got some blue-eyed babe watching his blind side. Pretty cute for an air cop, but I've got to admit, somewhat of a pro as well."

"Air cop, you say?" Grimaldi's eyes narrowed.

"Right. An SP sergeant. Knows her shit," Lyons said.

"And knows how to smoke Soviets for breakfast," Gadgets added with genuine respect. "You should have seen her go to town with Ironman's shotgun yesterday."

"They'll both be okay," Lyons said, ending the debate. "Now what have you got from the local police agencies?" he asked, changing the subject. "Anything?"

Lyons knew that Kurtzman and Grimaldi had been using the Bear's computer expertise to constantly scan not only airwaves popular with the Soviets' West Coast consulates, but also NASA's public and private ratio transmissions as well as those of the local police and sheriff's departments during the past ten hours. NASA's radio nets had been relatively quiet, but all it would take was one Russian attempt at tapping into the space agency's system, and Bear would stand a good chance of tracing Yuri the Ogre to his present safehouse.

"The only transmissions of any substance for the past four or five hours have regarded a bank robbery in Lompoc, and this...." Kurtzman handed over the data slip recently culled from his computer scan of information being put out and received by all law enforcement communication centers within a hundred mile radius of Vandenberg Air Force Base.

"A shoot-out at some joint called the Black Moon Saloon?" Lyons reread the card.

"Two police officers shot," he nodded. A civilian Medevac chopper they call 'Lifeguard One' airlifted 'em to an area hospital, but I heard its on-board flight nurse radio the emergency room about a probable DOA."

"Damn," Lyons muttered, flashing back to the years he'd put in with the LAPD and the dozen-odd funerals he'd attended before leaving the force. "Those poor guys...."

"That's not all," Grimaldi added, lifting a clipboard for Ironman's inspection. On it were scribbled the physical descriptions of two other corpses left behind at the shooting scene. Serial numbers and model types of the guns still clutched in their lifeless hands were also listed.

"East-Bloc." Lyons frowned. "Two big Ukrainian types with East-Bloc peashooters."

"KGB?" Schwarz nudged him. "Or Spetsnaz?"

"I don't know, but I'd sure like to find out what they were up to at a redneck saloon in the middle of the—"

"Knock it off!" Kurtzman blurted out. "I've got something coming over the NASA band—interference of some sort. The rocket scientists at the Runway Seven hangars were running a routine test on the *Specter*'s prop payload when some sort of probe split their transmission right down the middle."

"And just what exactly does that mean?" Lyons asked, folding his arms across his chest, unimpressed.

"You said 'a probe.'" Schwarz leaned closer to the communications console. "Get a trace on that sucker! Is it still transmitting?"

"I've already isolated the power source," Kurtzman said as he whirled around in his wheelchair and began flipping dials and switches on a tracking device mounted in the van's opposite wall.

Lyons listened to a tiny fiberglass radar beacon grinding against the van's roof overhead as it began twirling. Constructed of a clear but nearly indestructible material, the dish positioned topside was hardly noticeable by passersby.

"The pak-sets!" Lyons yelled at Schwarz.

"You got it!" Gadget flew out of the van's side door and raced toward an Air Force gun-jeep that the two Able Team commandos had been using for routine transportation about the base.

In a few seconds, he was sprinting back toward the minivan, a small portable radio in one hand. Once inside, he handed the sturdy Motorola four-channel to Lyons.

"Can you give me an approximate location?" Ironman demanded of Kurtzman.

"In the vicinity of Lake Guadalupe."

"Where?"

"A small community north of the base, just below the junction where PCH intersects with Highway 166." 'PCH' was local California jargon for the Pacific Coast Highway, which ran from Mexico to Canada. "About five clicks west of Santa Maria."

"They've got an airport there," Grimaldi advised everyone.

"Here—" Lyons placed the pak-set on top of the desk in front of Bear "—we're en route. When you can pinpoint the exact location of that transmitter, advise us over this pak-set."

"But I could—"

"I don't want you using the main net here," Lyons said, anticipating Kurtzman's objection. "Ogorodnikova might also have some sophisticated equipment at his disposal, and I don't want him intercepting any of your transmissions to us. With pak-sets, we're talking definite power fade, and a better chance of closing in on the Ogre without being detected.''

"You also might get completely out of range of this little portable," Grimaldi argued, "and find yourselves up shit creek."

"We've been there before," Ironman replied. "And we'll cross that obstacle if and when we come to it." Then he was following Gadgets back out the door, into a crimson dusk.

Jack Grimaldi's eyes followed them as they jumped into the M-60-equipped gun-jeep and sped toward the nearby west gate. From there, it would be north toward Lake Guadalupe. But for now, Gadgets and the Ironman were racing straight into the sizzling red sunset.

"Watch your ass, gentlemen," the covert pilot muttered under his breath, too softly for either commando to hear. "'Cause no one else's going to be there to cover you."

"For now," Aaron Kurtzman added cryptically.

"Is that what I think it is?"

"Looks like it," the Bear said as he reached for a telephone receiver and began dialing a complicated series of coded numbers.

"Very sneaky," Grimaldi sighed as he watched the detection equipment monitoring a computer scan that was taking place several miles away—at the space shuttle hangar on Runway Seven.

"This is Stony Man," Kurtzman's voice boomed across the telephone lines. "Priority C as in Charlie. I repeat: C as in Charlie. Right. Verify: Alpha Bravo Lima Echo. Right! Now patch me through to your CAD system," the Bear directed. "Then interface with NASA's data banks here at Vandenberg and link up with Pacific Bell—request their security department, ask for Operator Fourteen.'' Kurtzman paused, then snapped, ''What? Hell no! *Get on it!*'' he demanded. *''Now!''*

''I don't get it,'' Grimaldi complained. ''First the radio scramble...now this. What's going on?''

''Our friend Yuri the Ogre is getting desperate. He's attempting to tap in to the shuttle's computer banks via the public phone lines, which is next to impossible, thanks to NASA safeguards,'' Bear explained. ''He's attempting to program both *Specter* and the *Enterprise* to recognize and accept satellite commands via that Skylink contraption Brognola warned us about.''

''What about the *Atlantis*? Why isn't he trying to screw that up?'' Grimaldi demanded.

''I don't know!'' Kurtzman yelled back as he frantically twisted at frequency knobs and scanned radio channels. ''Maybe he is, and we just haven't detected the attempt. Anything's possible, you know—*Atlantis* is in Earth orbit, not on the ground. It's not like I have access to the Pentagon or NORAD!'' he complained, lifting his hands in the air, gesturing to the confining walls of the van.

''I know...I know, Bear—sorry! Just hang in there. Get what info you can. Ignore my blasted meddling. I'll shut up. I promise.''

A red light began flashing in the middle of the console, but abruptly went out. ''What was that?'' Grimaldi asked, unable to remain silent for long.

''NASA's routine antihacker safeguards have confronted the electronic probe and scrambled it, preventing computer-bank penetration and making useless and undecipherable any information the probe *might* have obtained prior to detection. The phone connection is now being terminated. It was a stupid attempt on Ogorodnikova's part in the first place.''

''But—'' Grimaldi raised a hand in muted protest.

"Not to fear—" Kurtzman waved the pilot silent "—NASA's equipment will keep the line path open despite breaking the actual audio connection—if you can understand that. The computers are running a trace through Pacific Bell's data banks at this time, and I'd say that in a few moments..."

The Bear went silent, cupping the headset against his right ear tightly. "Yes, go ahead, Lieutenant," he spoke into the mouthpiece. "What? Oh, shit," he sighed. "All right, I authenticate: Alpha Bravo Lima Echo—okay? Then go ahead. Ah, yes...that's it...thank you very much, Lieutenant.

"That was fast." Pen in hand, Bear began scribbling an address across a notepad.

"*What* was fast?" Grimaldi demanded to know.

"The probe originated at this address," he answered as he tore off a piece of paper and handed it to the pilot. "1286 Monterey Street, in Lake Guadalupe, California. Phone company claims it's a single-family dwelling. Police department confirms it."

"You just earned your dog food for the day, Bear!" Grimaldi patted the communications genius on the shoulder as he reached for the portable radio Lyons had left with them. "Jackster to Dodge City," he spoke into the pak-set.

A scratchy reply immediately came over the radio net. "Send it." Simple and to the point. Lyons's voice.

"Your target is at one-two-eight-six Monterey Street in the town of Lake Guadalupe, Ironman."

"Directions," came the next metallic transmission. It was not a request.

"Take Pacific Coast Highway north until you see the lights of Santa Maria on your right, about five miles out across the prairie—on the eastern horizon. It'll be your first major population center.

"As soon as you see it, you'll also be cruising adjacent to a large body of water. On the northern banks is Lake Guadalupe, population about 600 or so, over."

"Roger. Anything further?"

"You'll be looking for a one-family house on the east side of the road, twelve blocks up from the lake. Monterey Street runs north and south. Unknown on the color and any other particulars about the structure itself."

"Roger your last, Jackster."

"Keep a low profile, guys," Grimaldi added before ending the transmission. There was no reply over the radio. And he had not expected one.

19

Yuri Ogorodnikova raced from window to window, checking the property that surrounded his tri-level safehouse. The sophisticated equipment set up inside the largely vacant structure was revealing that his attempt at scrambling the backup computers housed aboard the *Specter* and *Enterprise* had been detected. The data being sent into space—and directed at the USS *Atlantis*—was most likely being diverted and traced as well. It would only be a matter of time before NASA notified Air Force Intelligence and the FBI to send their agents to Lake Guadalupe for early spring cleaning that would sterilize 1286 Monterey Street.

The Ogre picked up his telephone and dialed the Soviet consulate in Los Angeles. The phone on the other end rang over ten times before a gruff voice responded. "Yuri?" it asked tentatively.

"Yes, Dimitri." For the first time in decades, Ogorodnikova was unable to hide the fear in his voice. "I have..." He spoke in English, thinking that might mask his concerns, but he doubted the rotund bureaucrat at Depot One would be unable to detect it.

"You have trouble."

"Yes, Dimitri. Everything is going wrong. The U.S. government...they've sent in some madman commando outfit to disrupt our mission."

"The Spetsnaz frogmen were annihilated on the beach shortly after coming ashore."

"Yes."

"What kind of bungled operation *was* that, Yuri?"

"I don't know. They made mistakes, they were out-gunned—I just don't know."

"I had a nephew in that team of Special Forces sappers, Yuri."

"I'm sorry, Comrade Dimitri, I'm so very sorry to hear—"

"His name is Vasili Yeltis."

Yuri noted that Dimitri did not use the word *was*. "I'm sure he—"

"One of our sappers survived the American ambush, Yuri," Dimitri cut him off. "Find out if it was Vasili."

"Yes, I will, I will, Dimitri . . . but what about—"

"Whoever survived the blundered raid talked. If it was my nephew, I want you to dispose of him without delay."

"Yes, yes, Dimitri—I understand. I mean . . . but what about—" Yuri wiped perspiration from his forehead as he was interrupted again.

"You are in need of additional men?" The bureaucrat in Los Angeles sounded bored.

"Yes, Dimitri. My two best agents were killed in a shoot-out with police. I only have three men left, and I don't think they're much of a match for the elite squad of commandos that wiped out our team on the beach."

"You're on your own, Yuri."

"What?" Ogorodnikova demanded, flabbergasted.

"Too much energy has been expended on this ill-fated project from the start. It was a risky venture. It has not panned out. The planners are at this very moment being reassigned to outposts on the Nordvik frontier. Henceforth, you are on your own."

"*What?*"

"If you make it out of there, Yuri, report to the embassy in San Francisco at zero-six hundred sharp, tomorrow morning. We will have another... assignment for you."

"But what about the space shuttle *Atlantis*?"

"Moscow will take care of the Americans' orbiter. Your cell of insurgents has become an embarrassment to the Party, Yuri. Do not make things worse by—how do the American imperialists say it?—by 'rocking the boat.'"

Dimitri did not immediately hang up, and as Ogorodnikova listened to the dead silence consuming the line, he tried to picture the obese paper-pusher's face. Dimitri had not worked the street in decades. He issued directives; people died. That was all.

"I assume you are telling me that I cannot expect any immediate help from Los Angeles," Yuri the Ogre spoke slowly, in precise English.

"Not from Los Angeles, *or* San Francisco. Not even from Mother Russia, Yuri." Dimitri coughed into his mouthpiece, and Ogorodnikova harbored a secret desire that the big Soviet would choke to death on his own words. "You've reached the end of the line, as our beloved Americans like to say. Now is the time for you to prove yourself to those at the Kremlin. And to me."

"But Dimitri..."

"This is your last chance, my friend. Literally."

And the line between Lake Guadalupe and downtown Los Angeles went dead.

"LISTEN TO THIS," the man huddled in a wheelchair, reading a newspaper, said to the man polishing his aviator sunglasses. "John Denver tried to get NASA to let him go on one of the upcoming space shuttle missions."

"John Denver the 'Rocky Mountain High' singer?"

"Roger."

"I suppose he wanted to compose a tune about circling the earth in zero gravity or something."

"I suppose," the handicapped veteran replied. "Anyway, NASA turned him down, so Johnny-san beats feet to the Soviets, requesting the same thing: passenger status aboard an upcoming flight of their Russian version of the shuttle, *Kosmolet*. And the Commies said 'no sweat' and 'can do' to the dude."

"You're kidding."

"But there's a price tag attached. The Ruskies want ten million for the round-trip ticket. And that's up front."

"Is he gonna pay?"

"It doesn't say."

A red light over one of the many phones hanging from the communications bank in front of the two men began flashing, and the wheelchair-bound genius picked up the receiver at the first ring.

"It's for you." Aaron Kurtzman handed the phone to Jack Grimaldi.

"Nobody knows I'm here," Grimaldi said, refusing to take the receiver at first.

"He asked for 'our infamous airborne man.' And that's you."

Grimaldi's posture straightened noticeably the moment he realized who he was speaking to. "Yes, Chief?"

Kurtzman watched the pilot's facial expressions change from being surprised to excited to indifferent as he listened to Hal Brognola on the other end. "Yes sir...yes sir, you've got it."

Finally Grimaldi handed the phone back to Kurtzman. "Whew!" he said. "Things are really beginning to move fast, my friend."

"How so?" Kurtzman placed the receiver to his ear, heard a dial tone, and replaced it on a plastic hook protruding from the communications console.

"That was the Chief," Grimaldi explained unnecessarily. "He just got off the red phone with some diplomat at the Soviet consulate in L.A."

"Don't tell me...." Bear rolled his eyes up in their sockets until only the white bottoms were visible.

"It's not what you think," Jack said, pointing at the portable radio Lyons had left them. "Get on the horn to Ironman. The KGB has disowned Yuri the Ogre."

"What?" Kurtzman demanded as he immediately grabbed the pak-set, turned up the volume and clicked off the squelch for additional power.

"Yeah! Brognola says that it's now open season on Ogorodnikova and whoever's inside the safehouse. Our not-so-beloved KGB field agent has gone rabid, threatening to cause an international incident. He's been telephoning every Soviet politician and diplomat in California, claiming the San Francisco desk has cast him out in the cold. And Yuri the Ogre is refusing to stand down, surrender his weapons or cancel his mission. The Russians at 1286 Monterey Street are now considered to be a renegade faction of the KGB and a definite threat to the space shuttle *Atlantis*."

"Did his superiors admit to what Yuri's mission *was*— or is that a stupid question and wishful thinking on my part?" Kurtzman kept busy, working with over a dozen, eight-channel police scanners plugged into his monitoring headset.

Grimaldi did not seek to embarrass the Bear. "Air Force Intelligence and NASA Security has also zeroed in on our Monterey Street tri-level at Lake Guadalupe," he revealed. "They say three or four radio transmissions have emanated from a satellite dish attached to the roof of the house. And that the dish is tracking the USS *Atlantis*—if you can picture *that*."

"Do they have any idea why?" A look of intense worry creased Kurtzman's brow. "I mean, do they think these guys actually have the ability to bring down the orbiter?''

"There's the chance Ogorodnikova and our Colonel Lynch succeeded in compromising the entire shuttle program. Until the *Atlantis* lands at Vandenberg tomorrow morning...."

"Or crashes into the desert," Kurtzman interjected without enthusiasm.

"We'll just have to wait and see." Grimaldi stared down at the pak-set and pressed the transmit lever with his thumb. "Jackster to Dodge City."

"Send it, Big G," came the static-laced reply.

"Ironman, I've got good news, and I've got bad news...."

"GET THE CAR READY!" Ogorodnikova screamed at the semicircle of veteran KGB agents gathered in the hallway outside his cluttered office. Had they overheard his conversation with Dimitri in Los Angeles or the other sector heads in consulates across California? It didn't matter. These men hated the latest Soviet bureaucracy as much as he did. They would side with Yuri the Ogre through thick and thin. Of that he harbored few doubts.

There were five men in the semicircle. Five men and one woman.

The female, her long chestnut hair tucked up under a chauffeur's cap, darted toward the back door, heading for the Citroen parked outside.

Yuri had purposefully deceived Dimitri as to the number of survivors of his team. Yuri had felt that if the KGB section chief in Los Angeles thought Ogorodnikova had only two or three men, he'd rush reinforcements to Lake Guadalupe. But the senior field agent had been wrong.

With several KGB vets escorting him, he just might make it out of this alive, Yuri decided.

"You! Nikita!" he called to one of the men. "Help me destroy the equipment in the computer room downstairs! I want two people to the front windows, two to the rear. Keep and eye out for—"

"It is too late!" the attractive Ukrainian woman with the chestnut hair claimed as she rushed back into the room, a Tokarev 7.62 revolver in her hand. There was no doubt in Ogorodnikova's mind that she was deadly accurate with the gun. And accurate about her observations outside, as well. "They're arriving now!" she said, confirming his worst fears without preamble. "In a jeep with machine guns mounted in the back!"

"But they are not Air Force police!" Nikita called from beside the front window. "They are dressed entirely in black! Commandos of some sort."

"I told you to go to the computer room!" Yuri raged. "Start smashing everything that has a hard disk in it. *Now!*"

The KGB boss then rushed over to the window and stared out at the fading twilight gloom. "Svetlana!" he called to the female agent. "Start the car! Leave it running, then get back in here! If they swing around back while you're out there, shoot the three men—shoot to kill!"

"Yes, Yuri!" She dashed back out the door, never pausing to question his directive.

Smoke began billowing from the computer room in the basement as Nikita—the agent destroying sensitive communications gear—set off several thermite charges.

"Fool!" Ogorodnikova screamed toward the stairwell. "No meltdown bombs until we abandon this place!"

"It is too late!" both agents standing by the rear window yelled as smoke filled the house's ground-floor level. Once the thermite bombs were ignited, there was very little that could be done to stop them from melting through metal, aluminum, wood or tile—the solid chemical burned through almost anything placed in front of, beside or below it.

"Damn!" Ogorodnikova muttered as Nikita stumbled up out of the cellar, gagging on the smoke despite the gas mask covering his face.

Yuri tore the mask off and punched the Russian in the stomach. "You fool!" he chastised. "You should have waited until we were ready to leave! I just wanted you to start breaking consoles and disk-drives at this point! The other data banks could have waited!"

At that moment, a burst of red tracers smashed through the living room window, ending the one-sided conversation.

20

Lake Guadalupe was a small town, nestled in a common, unimpressive stretch of flatlands that ran for miles along the north and west banks of the body of water from which the town got its name. The streets were laid out in tidy grid fashion, with no diagonal or meandering avenues or trails. Everything ran north and south or east and west.

The homes in the twelve hundred block of Monterey Street were two-story and tri-level affairs in the eighty thousand dollar range—cheap by Southern California standards. Lake Guadalupe's isolated location probably accounted for the low real estate values.

Huge trees rose up along the banks of the lake, and the homes there were shaded from the same sun that baked the nearby dry-salt lake beds. Farther north, where Yuri Ogorodnikova had chosen to rent his group's safehouse, there was only sparse vegetation, however. The yards were large, composed mostly of crabgrass and decorative rock, and surrounded by low picket fences or, in many cases, no fences at all.

The house at 1286 Monterey Street *did* boast a high chain-link fence—taller than most adult males—but there was no sagging barbed wire running along the fence posts, and the front double gate was almost always open.

The neighbors were not overly curious about Ogorodnikova and his assortment of foreign-looking and Russian-speaking friends. As long as one occupant was present—the attractive girl with long, chestnut hair—the neighbors never voiced any objections to so many men sharing the house.

Not that they didn't have their suspicions, which were routinely voiced at Big Bob's corner barbershop. But the bent-over old man, who most often entered and left the house, always kept the yard tidy and was never without a nod, wave or kind word for the elderly widowed ladies residing on the block.

So it was quite a shock to some, but not to others, that all hell broke loose on the eve of NASA's much-heralded launch of the space shuttle *Atlantis* only a few miles to the south.

It was the night Monterey Street became a free-fire zone.

And Able Team was part of all the ruckus.

Lyons and Schwarz could have waited for Blancanales. They could have called in the Air Cavalry, complete with gunships and Jolly Green Giants—not to mention the Security Police. They might even have played it conservatively by surrounding Yuri Ogorodnikova's safehouse with representatives of the local law enforcement agencies.

But Able Team's crack commandos rarely operated that way. Hal Brognola had directed them to do a job: isolate, confine, then terminate the renegade faction of KGB agents. Without fanfare. And as quietly as possible.

Assaulting Ogorodnikova's safehouse with an M-60 gun-jeep was not exactly charging into a tense situation in a low-key manner, but there was no sense taking too many chances, Ironman rationalized. But the ex-L.A. cop didn't feel he needed official reinforcements, either. Gadgets behind the steering wheel, and Lyons's own trusty fists manning the heavy machine gun mounted in the jeep's back seat, would suffice.

Ironman sent over a hundred 7.62 mm bullets into the house on their first pass alone. Swinging around the tri-level in a counterclockwise direction—much of the time on two wheels—Schwarz kept the Soviets' heads turning as he floored the gas pedal. The gun-jeep's spinning rear tires sent dust billowing throughout the front and back yards, creating an effective smoke screen from which to work.

The house's front and rear windows glowed with muzzle-flashes as the KGB agents inside opened up on the SP jeep with assault rifles and large-caliber handguns.

Schwarz swerved wildly back and forth, making the jeep a difficult target to hit, but it was not hard to simply spray an entire banana clip of AK-47 rounds at the two brazen Americans.

Green and Orange tracers danced along the jeep's rear bumper, throwing sparks on Gadgets's back. Lyons reached down and slapped the smoldering flak jacket several times, but had to resume holding on to the hog-60's handles as Schwarz ignored the burns eating into his back and continued driving reckless circles around the safehouse.

On the third pass by the front yard, the windows seemed to be filled with twice as many gunshot flashes. Some of the KGB agents were firing two weapons now— one in each hand. The increase in enemy lead did not greatly concern Ironman, however. Gadgets was a great driver under fire, and almost all of the bright barrel flames appeared long and streaklike, which meant, more often than naught, that the hot slugs were going to miss their mark. Elongated muzzle-flashes revealed that the weapon was being fired at an angle and therefore not directly at the Ironman or Schwarz. It was the round, glowing dots in the night one had to worry about: small circles of exploding light meant you were looking straight down the gun barrel when it was fired. And *that* could prove unhealthy as hell.

"Time to party!" Lyons said reaching into a canteen cover riding his hip. It did not hold a water jug however—Ironman used the cloth pouch to carry a handful of M-26 frags. Six of the grenades, to be precise. Crouching in the backseat, he pulled two safety pins with his teeth and, aiming for a side window, heaved both devices.

Gadgets chose to resume zigzagging at that point, however, and both grenades bounced off a window ledge and into the front doorway's fancy foyer.

Dual explosions sent elaborate brass molding out into the front yard. Pain-laced screams echoed from within the house as a blanket of dense smoke settled over the lawn.

Lyons threw the remaining grenades at the rear door on two subsequent passes, and by then the gun-jeep's tires had been shot to shreds. It was running on rims, and throwing a fountain of sparks out against the creeping night each time Gadgets raced across the front circular drive and rear walkway.

A fire had erupted in the basement computer room—that was evident from the intense glow visible through the shrapnel-damaged seams of the house—and as the vicious inferno filled the building with dense smoke, plumes of the inky stuff drove a small, wiry Russian out onto the front porch just as Gadgets was bringing the gun-jeep within a few feet of the foyer.

Unable to wing the M-60 around far enough on its beam swivel, Lyons temporarily abandoned the heavy weapon and drew his revolver.

The .357 Magnum's hammer dropped once, and a hollowpoint slug split the short KGB agent's face down the middle just as he was trying to reach out and press his rifle's muzzle against Schwarz's head before pulling the trigger.

The Russian slumped back against a porch swing, and his AK-47 jerked skyward. The dying man's finger refused to let up on the trigger and thirty rounds of brilliant white tracer rose up into the night sky in a broad arc before the magazine emptied itself and the bolt locked back on an empty chamber.

"Look out!" Lyons yelled, as another Soviet, his clothes and hair on fire, bolted from the front door and sprinted across the lawn, directly into the gun-jeep's path. The KGB agent's lips began crackling as he ran into the warm breeze, and they too burst into a glowing flame, peeling back away from shattered teeth.

Ironman brought the M-60 around, planning to send a burst of big slugs into the Russian's back—putting the man out of his misery—but a massive blast erupted from inside the safehouse. Searing waves of heat rolled out across the ground, catching the gun-jeep's left side, and as Gadgets fought to maintain control of the steering wheel, he overcorrected.

"Hold on to your haunches!" Lyons yelled as the jeep flipped over onto its side, slid through the grass for several yards then crashed into a parked car and rolled onto its top.

The gun-jeep lay slightly at an angle—the M-60's tall support beam had kept the vehicle from crushing its two occupants much as a roll bar would. Beside the jeep, what remained of a new Mercedes now hissed and groaned. Its entire left side was crushed.

Shards of jagged metal from the luxury auto protruded into the gun-jeep, effectively pinning the men from Stony Man Farm to the ground for several seconds—until they were able to kick the warped quarter panels and peeled-off doors away with the bottoms of their boots.

Gas was pouring from shrapnel holes in the fuel tank, however, and before either Lyons or Schwarz could free themselves from the twisted metal, they were both completely soaked in the flammable liquid. Sirens in the distance reached their ears then. "Cops?" Schwarz yelled hopefully as flames moved slowly across the dry lawn.

Skilled at distinguishing siren pitch, Lyons shook his head from side to side. "Fire fighters!" he said. "The neighbors probably called them. And not a minute too soon!"

A new voice volunteered an unwanted comment then.

"Too late for *you*, my friend...."

His revolver lying in the grass several feet away, Lyons reacted instantly to the Soviet accent. Drawing the seven-inch dagger from its thigh sheath, he flung the blade in a powerful, underhanded throw in the direction of the voice.

Groaning as soon as they were struck, two KGB agents dropped to their knees. The agent in the foreground, clutched at his throat, which had been sliced open by the blade halfway through its travels; the other had been unlucky enough to be standing directly behind the first Russian.

After slashing the first man's carotid artery, jugular vein and esophagus the heavy commando dagger flipped in a wobbly spiral, end over end through the air, finally implanting itself in the second agent's left eye. He lost more than his vision.

"What kind of lucky, hotshot softball throw was that?" Schwarz, Able Team's baseball enthusiast, asked.

"See you in hell, Gadgets!" Lyons muttered as he resumed working frantically to free himself.

Schwarz was not laughing as he kicked viciously at the planks of iron pinning him against the jeep's dashboard.

"Watch out!" Lower torso still pinned, Schwarz crossed both hands over his face defensively as Yuri the Ogre bolted from the burning house—a Russian SKS carbine in both hands.

He rushed directly for the overturned jeep, firing three-round bursts from the hip. Dirt flew up from the lawn stretching between Ogorodnikova and the helpless Americans as he stumbled over a body.

But before Yuri could regain his balance and correct his aim, a blinding burst of red tracers slammed into the clavicle over his left breast, whirling the KGB agent around as it knocked him off his feet.

Ogorodnikova was not finished yet, however. The wounds were not fatal. He struggled to his feet and staggered around the corner of the house, into the flame-brightened backyard, as Lyons and Schwarz strained to see who fired the cluster of M-16 rounds.

An earsplitting screech filled their ears suddenly as Sergeant Pamela Pearce slid up to the gun-jeep on her knees, fire extinguisher in hand. White foam soon covered Schwarz's face.

"You two just can't stay out of trouble, can you?" she yelled as several more SP trucks skidded up to the scene.

"Where the heck did *you* come from?" Lyons demanded as flashing lights atop the emergency vehicles bathed the yard with hot red and blue beams.

"No time to explain all that!" Pearce said as she waved one of the quarter-ton Alert Team vehicles up to the overturned gun-jeep. "Are either of you badly injured?"

"Just pinned to the ground!" Schwarz yelled. "Get this pile of scrap metal *off* us!"

"Your wish is granted!" Pearce offered a casual salute with one hand as she waved the SP truck closer with the other. Then she was off again, firing short, controlled bursts of copper-jacketed slugs through the thick columns of black smoke pouring from the glowing house's windows.

Metal screeched in protest, and safety glass crackled as the gun-jeep was forced off the two commandos clad in black and on to its side.

"It don't get much closer than that!" Lyons said about their canceled rendezvous with Lady Death.

"Screw it!" Gadgets returned, lifting an M-16 from the debris and throwing it to Ironman as he located a blood-stained AK-47 for his own use. "Let's go!"

Within minutes they had joined the air cops and had, in fact, found Ogorodnikova and the Russian woman. She had escorted her leader into the silver Citroen as blood squirted in weak spurts from his left shoulder and chest area. The foreign sedan had been secreted between two giant oak trees behind the house, out of sight.

The woman's cap had fallen off somewhere, and her radiant hair now cascaded down over bare shoulders where her blouse had been ripped into shreds during the firefight.

Her eyes glowed with hate as she glanced back at the Americans closing in on the Citroen. She wanted revenge and she wanted it bad.

"Get them!" Lyons yelled at Blancanales, who was fighting side-by-side with Sergeant Tuskin, and was now closest to the old man and his former chauffeur.

Two Russians brandishing Uzis burst through the house's front doors as Ironman spoke. They immediately opened fire on the Able Team warriors.

Sergeant Pearce killed them both instantly with head hits.

The Citroen's back quarter panels were already riddled with bullet holes. The license plate was gone—probably shot off by the gun-jeep during Lyons's and Schwarz's first roaring pass in the vehicle. Now the car's rear tires began spinning across the blood-slick grass as the Russian woman thrust the gearshift into low, pulling away from the concealment of the trees.

"Damn!" Lyons yelled, aiming at the Citroen. He pulled up on his M-16 at the last moment, jacking a round into the sky—Blancanales had darted into his field of fire without warning, nearly buying the farm with cash.

Lyons did not want this thing to escalate into a high-speed pursuit. He wanted the whole escapade to end right there.

Twice he had the woman in his sights as the Citroen skidded sideways through the patch of lawn connecting the backyard with the front, but a number of SPs, attempting to help, bobbed about in his line of fire. They prevented a clean shot.

Three sharp, abrupt whistles reached Lyons's ears then and, recognizing Gadgets's signal, he shifted his avenue of approach to the right as Blancanales came around on the far side of the house. The warrior's M-60 machine gun was cradled in muscular arms that were smeared with gun oil and an honest man's sweat.

As Pol concentrated on the Citroen, spraying a forty-round sustained burst into the fishtailing sedan's front engine compartment, Gadgets directed his attention at two more soot-faced men who had appeared on the front porch, blazing away with handguns.

Allowing his slung AK to drop sideways against his body, Schwarz drew his holstered Beretta and pulled the trigger a smooth half dozen times without pausing to raise the pistol to chest height or aim. The renowned expert on quiet-kill and urban guerrilla tactics merely allowed his hand to follow, by reflex, his line of sight. Gadgets trusted his battle-honed instincts implicitly.

The Beretta 93-R Schwarz carried had been modified for Able Team use with a suppressor and machined springs that silenced the weapon by allowing the cycling of subsonic 9 mm cartridges. An added flash suppressor further supplemented the weapon's prowess as a silent killer. Three blowgunlike discharges erupted. They were barely noticeable amid all the other gunfire and shouts, and one of the KGB agents flew backward through what remained of the house's huge picture window.

Ignoring the crackling of collapsing glass shards, Gadgets's eyes shifted to the second KGB agent, who had not even seemed to notice his partner's fate, and was taking aim on the nearest Air Force SP. Gadgets's gun hand again followed the line of sight movement.

Still holding his breath from the last three-round burst, Schwarz drew the trigger in again. He could not resist grinning at the professional results. The first bullet snapped the Russian's arm at the wrist, sending a fine spray of blood onto his shirt and trousers. The resulting collage of crimson-on-white resembled a modern art print from a Rodeo Drive gallery more than the ugly fruits of a rural shoot-out. The second round knocked the pistol from his hand as he grabbed at the shredded tendons, trying desperately to staunch the flow of blood. The impact from the powerful slug whirled the KGB agent around just as the third struck him in the right thigh, inflicting a compound fracture to the upper leg bone, which splintered and burst forth through both flesh and fabric with a gut-flopping *rip*!

While Schwarz and Lyons dealt with the Soviet gunmen, Blancanales concentrated on the speeding Citroen. He raced around to the front of the sedan and unleashed the last of his belt of machine-gun rounds directly into the radiator, just as Ironman appeared less than ten meters away.

Lyons delivered a devastating body block to three KGB agents clustered at the foot of the front porch, who appeared to be waiting for the fishtailing Citroen to slide close again so they could hop in. A squad of rifle-waving SPs were quickly standing over the Ironman, eager to take the Soviets into custody—once they recovered from having the breath knocked out of them by the ex-college linebacker.

Schwarz appeared beside the Citroen as Blancanales finally succeeded in killing the car's motor. Grinning, Gadgets brought his pistol barrel slowly up—until it was pointing directly at the young woman seated behind the steering wheel.

The woman knew she was outclassed and outgunned—both hands slowly rose up off the steering wheel in surrender.

Schwarz rushed around to the side of the car, grabbed hold of her wrists and tied them to the outer door handle with a pair of flexicuffs he removed from inside his belt.

He quickly inspected the Citroen's interior and found Yuri Ogorodnikova lying on the floorboards in the back seat, semiconscious and apparently bleeding to death from his gunshot wound.

"I could use a medic over here!" Gadgets called out halfheartedly. "Then again," he muttered under his breath, "it'd be no big loss one way or the other."

When he glanced back to gauge the progress of Blancanales and Lyons, he was not surprised to find that the balance of Able Team had succeeded in disarming the last of Yuri the Ogre's bodyguards without firing additional shots. Pol was sitting on a KGB agent's head as Lyons attempted to twist the man's arms back so that he could apply a set of flexicuffs.

At that moment, Sergeant Pamela Pearce moved her van into the yard, skidding up dramatically to the fracas as curious onlookers from the neighboring homes parted to let a convoy of wailing fire trucks pass through.

The rear doors of Pearce's van promptly popped open from inside, and several more security policemen jumped out as the original team of haggard-looking SPs began escorting prisoners over to the vehicle. "Clear that house before the fire fighters move in!" she directed. "Room-to-room, gentlemen! Now let's hustle before it gets dangerous around here!"

"Who's got the body bags?" someone yelled.

BEFORE THE FIRE was brought under control—or the dust even settled—Pearce had her vehicle's rear tires spinning again. Back to the stockade at Vandenberg. Back to the real world—where numbers and quotas and stats counted most. Much like prisoners of war.

Schwarz watched the van race along the road that paralleled Lake Guadalupe. The enemy who were not headed for an interrogation cubicle and federal prison, would spend quite a while on some hospital jail ward. *Then* they'd get a free, one-way ticket to the big Monkey House at Leavenworth.

The van's rear doors were still open—swinging wildly back and forth—and Ironman leaned out through the back just when Gadgets expected he might. The ex-cop raised a clenched fist, immediately locking eyes with Schwarz without having to search him out. Two fingers of the fist flew up into a meaty V.

Gadgets knew the Ironman's gesture was for victory.

21

Before he died, Yuri the Ogre revealed the location of the Skylink device, confirming Lynch's message from low Earth orbit. He also told the men of Able Team that the satellite relay switching device had been reprogrammed to scramble the complicated, computer-operated hydraulics system aboard space shuttle *Atlantis*, as well as impede other critical controls and safeguards secreted within the orbiter's command module. Colonel Lynch's attempts at countermanding the directives would have been wasted if Skylink had activated itself. The exact method of reprogramming made it next to impossible for any scientist outside the KGB circle of influence to countermand the microwave directives once they were transmitted. Skylink would have to be destroyed, Ogorodnikova insisted. Before it came to life. It was the only way.

And why was the Soviet agent betraying Moscow now? Ogorodnikova claimed it had a little something to do with a phone call from Comrade Dimitri, in Los Angeles, but he would not elaborate.

And then he died, without pomp and circumstance, broken and bitter.

One thing Ogorodnikova did *not* reveal to Lyons and the others was that Skylink was rigged with a powerful self-destruct charge of plastic explosive, which would detonate instantly should anyone without the proper access codes attempt to tamper with the device. Dimitri was the only other man on earth who possessed that code.

Gadgets Schwarz may have been born at night, but not *last* night. He had suspected that Skylink was rigged to a detonating device of some sort all along, and programmed to explode rather than fall into American hands.

It now fell to Able Team to get to the device and blow it in place—before *Atlantis* descended for its dawn landing at Vandenberg Air Force Base. If Lyons and his people could dismantle the C-4 explosive packet and remove the detonating device intact, they would be able to present Military Intelligence with an advanced piece of Soviet technology: Skylink.

Hal Brognola was in no mood for the antics of aspiring heroes, however: he immediately dispatched an Air Force bomb-disposal squad to assist in the operation. But, first, it would be up to Able Team to locate Skylink.

The predawn raid conducted by Lyons, Schwarz and Blancanales took on a tense urgency as the first signs of pale pink light began spreading along the eastern horizon. They had spent the past two hours scouring the cliffs where Colonel Lynch had been detailed by Pearce's SAT team over two weeks earlier—inspecting crevices and bushes with metal detectors—but to no avail.

It was Gadgets who finally stumbled across the device—and "stumble" is putting it lightly.

He and Lyons were slowly crossing a narrow ledge some two hundred feet above the dry lake bed when the weak shale outcropping beneath Schwarz's boots gave way, and he plummeted down toward a solitary slab of rare igneous rock jutting into thin air far below.

On the trip down, he grabbed on to everything he could find, including shrubs, cacti and a startled sidewinder snake. Hands filled with thorns and clumps of sagebrush, he frantically flung the hissing reptile away, lost his balance again, and dropped another fifty feet into a deep crevice.

It took Lyons and the others nearly a half hour to reach him. While he was waiting, a gust of wind caused two sheets of camouflage tarp behind a nearby boulder to whip at the cool, predawn air.

Gadgets investigated and found Skylink reclining on its tripod, nestled in the pit Colonel Lynch had dug—its antenna dish pointed toward the boiling orb of crimson snow struggling to rise above the eastern horizon.

The fact that the landing of the space shuttle *Atlantis* was running slightly behind schedule was what saved them—and the orbiter.

"Down here!" Schwarz screamed. "I found it! But it'll take too long to get an ordnance disposal team in on this ledge. I think we're gonna need—"

The rush of flapping rotors silenced Gadgets Schwarz.

A giant shadow blocked out the rising sun as a twin rotored Chinook appeared over the clifftop above, drifting directly above the Able Team commando's position.

Within seconds, four thick ropes dropped from the hovering ship's belly, and an equal number of highly trained experts from the Air Force's bomb squad began rappeling down through a hundred feet of morning mist to Gadgets's position.

"I wish I could tell you to stand back," a broad shouldered technical sergeant said. "But there doesn't appear to be much room for you to go anywhere!" He laughed as the three other NCOs landed with powerful squats and immediately set about removing probe and defusing equipment from their backpacks.

"Of course, you could flee the scene via one of these babies!" A tall, slender sergeant with stitches across one cheek held his rappeling rope out to Schwarz.

"No thanks," Gadgets answered, dropping into a crouch behind the three professionals. "If you don't mind, I'll stick around and watch."

"Never know when you'll have to diffuse one of these suckers on the job, right?" the first NCO snickered sarcastically.

Schwarz grew somber as he flashed back to the bloody carnage on Monterey Street in Lake Guadalupe, and the exploding house, the dismembered bodies littering the yard, the young Air Force SPs getting their first taste of gunplay. "Considering *my* line of work, pal, you don't know how right you are."

"That was easy," the NCO with the stitches crisscrossing his face said. He held an aluminum box—roughly six by eight inches rectangularly, and three-quarters of an inch thick—out away from Skylink with a pair of rubberized pliers. Wires dangled from a hole along one side.

The detonator and power pack.

"Hell, I've dismantled more sophisticated shit assembled by Victor Charlie, back in Nam," he boasted with an evil grin. "Them bomb builders over in Moscow are really losin' their touch. Gonna have to send Gorby some hate mail. Now who's gonna buy the first round of beers when we get back to Vandenberg?"

"Ain't she BEAU-tiful," the sergeant commented, motioning toward the eastern horizon. Descending swiftly now, like a falling star devoured by a burst of golden sun rays, *Atlantis* dropped from space, her protective anti-heat tiles glowing a bright red as she reentered the Earth's atmosphere, gliding toward the dry lake bed below.

"Quite a sight," the sergeant said. "Kind of reminds me of flares, drifting on the edge of Saigon all night long." He turned to face the Able Team commando. "You ever been to Nam, boy?"

Gadgets locked eyes with the bomb disposal expert and produced a haunting Death's Head grin, but the two men were not smiling about the same thing.

EPILOGUE

"I'm going to recommend that the Pentagon whitewash this thing as far as Colonel Paul Lynch's involvement goes," Hall Brognola advised the men of Able Team as they sat in Major Fletcher's Criminal Investigations office at Vandenberg Air Force Base.

Rosario Blancanales had just finished reading a telex Brognola handed to him, and, as instructed, was passing it along to Lyons—a telex which Air Force Intelligence had intercepted as it was on its way to the Soviet consulate in Los Angeles.

Gadgets Schwarz was sitting cross-legged on the floor, adjusting the reception on a small, portable television set the major kept in her cramped office. The set sat atop a much larger VCR. On the picture tube, a replay of the successful orbiter mission: USS *Atlantis* descending at dawn for a perfect landing on Runway Seven dry lake bed.

"This sucks," Lyons said, starting to wad up the telex.

"I need that for the file," Brognola stopped him.

"Screw the file," Ironman muttered, but he surrendered the telex without further protest.

"I said I'm going to recommend that Hawkjaw go down in the annals of Air Force history as a hero," Brognola repeated for Schwarz's benefit, but the electronics genius appeared immersed in the official Vandenberg videotape of the landing.

"We heard you, Chief." Gadgets glanced back over a shoulder and trained sad dog eyes on Brognola.

"After all," the Stony Man director of operations said, "Lynch cooperated with authorities in the end...."

"What authorities?" Major Fletcher spoke for the first time since closing the office doors.

"Captain Lourdes," Brognola revealed. "Lynch told him everything—or just about, anyway."

"Up in the shuttle." Blancanales locked eyes with her. "Astronaut Lynch confided in Astronaut Lourdes. Before he died. It was what helped us break this case. And bring *Atlantis* home."

"Well, the colonel shouldn't be exonerated," Fletcher maintained. "Too many dedicated security policemen died over this fiasco. It was just as much a tragedy as the *Challenger*—"

"How can you call that a fiasco?" Schwarz pointed to the videotape of *Atlantis* as she touched down in a picture-perfect landing just as the warming rays of sunrise broke free of the eastern horizon.

Refusing to enter into their argument, Brognola picked up the crumpled telex and read it for the tenth time. The message was confirmation that Colonel Lynch's Vietnamese wife had been dead for fourteen years. She committed suicide as Communist forces surged into Saigon.

Eyes sad with personal reflection as he thought of his own days working in Vietnam's City of Sorrows, the Stony Man chief's resolve—and faith in his fellow countrymen—was nevertheless bolstered somewhat as Gadgets reached forward and turned up the volume on the TV set.

He listened respectfully as the narrator reminded everyone in the room that *Atlantis*'s flight had been flawless—a glowing tribute to the crew of the *Challenger*, who so valiantly sacrificed their lives so that mankind's quest for conquering the unknown could continue.

The faces of that crew flashed across the screen as a rare tear formed along the edge of Hal Brognola's eye, refusing to slide down his cheek. Its presence remained proof positive the tough anticrime crusader had a soft spot in his heart for the astronauts of *Challenger*.

"Yes, it was a flawless flight," the narrator repeated, "with none of the outside interference military authorities had been reportedly concerned about. The entire mission went off with such precision—NASA's Mission Control claims—that there were few reminders of the *Challenger* tragedy of 1986.

"Yes, NASA's space program is back on track. The galaxies are once again within reach, it seems, beckoning to us with endless opportunities. The meek may inherit the earth, dear friends, but we proud Americans will venture forth to the stars and beyond!"

''Able Team will go anywhere, do anything, in order to complete their mission.''

—*West Coast Review of Books*

MEAN STREETS

SUPER ABLE TEAM #1
DICK STIVERS

The Desmondos, an organized street gang, terrorize the streets of Los Angeles armed with AK-47s and full-auto Uzis.

Carl Lyons and his men are sent in to follow the trail of blood and drugs to the power behind these teenage terrorists.

The Desmondos are bad, but they haven't met Able Team.

In Bolan's never-ending war against organized crime, the hunter has become the hunted. But the battle is only beginning.

DON PENDLETON's

MACK BOLAN

BLOWOUT

Framed for murder and wanted by both sides of the law, Bolan escapes into the icy German underground to stalk a Mafia-protected drug baron.

TAKE 'EM NOW

FOLDING SUNGLASSES FROM GOLD EAGLE

Mean up your act with these tough, street-smart shades. Practical, too, because they fold 3 times into a handy, zip-up polyurethane pouch that fits neatly into your pocket. Rugged metal frame. Scratch-resistant acrylic lenses. Best of all, they can be yours for only $6.99.

MAIL YOUR ORDER TODAY.

Send your name, address, and zip code, along with a check or money order for just $6.99 + .75¢ for postage and handling (for a total of $7.74) payable to Gold Eagle Reader Service. (New York and Iowa residents please add applicable sales tax.)

Remove from pouch

unfold once

GOLD EAGLE Gold Eagle Reader Service
901 Fuhrmann Blvd.
P.O. Box 1396
Buffalo, N.Y. 14240-1396

unfold twice

and they're ready to wear

GES-1A

Offer not available in Canada.